Mr. Chatter, with his gun still aimed at Leo, decided to keep talking. "At best you could get one of us before we gunned you down."

Laughing, I lifted my gun away from them slowly before dropping it.

The gun started to drop before stopping and floating into place pressed lightly against Mr. Mountain's forehead. "Do you have any idea where you are?"

Mr. Chatter took on a look of confusion, and for the first time since he had started talking, Mr. Chatter was speechless.

I crossed my arms over my chest. Holding the gun in place with my magic was more of a parlor trick than anything. Moving objects was one of the easier spells, but holding them in place for any length of time could be tiring. I hid it from my face as I spoke.

"This isn't the Dean's office in some random private university. This is Miskatonic University. It's the largest collection of volatile and arcane magics from all over the world!" I barked another laugh. "You are standing in a city that has been referred to as a hub for every vile creature that has roamed this planet!"

Mr. Chatter asked, "What does any of that even mean?" He shot a confused glance at his nearest companion.

"It means," I smiled, "that my local Wendigo is the most dedicated secretary in the business!"

Something vaguely human-shaped fell from the ceiling and onto Mr. Chatter. A fount of blood shot from the fast moving mass of Wendigo and Mr. Chatter. His companions only stared, terrified by the sight before them.

ANDREW DORAN

At the Mountains of Madness

by Matthew Davenport

For Mike. Have an adventure.

Chapter 1: Utah

Utah, in the summer months, is Hell.

In a heated gun battle, I chased a small group of Nazis across the Utah desert to a small train station about three miles from a now smoldering ruin of a shack that once belonged to the missing Professor William Dyer.

I went to Utah in search of Dr. Dyer, the famed geologist of Miskatonic University. It took me a week to find his niece who was kind enough to give me directions to his summer cabin in Utah. Geologists love their rocks, and the formations near his cabin were some of the most beautiful in the country.

When I found the cabin, I was already too late. William Dyer wasn't there, but three very trigger-happy Nazis were. They'd already started setting fire to the place, but I saw what I needed.

One of them was carrying a journal that I was certain didn't belong to him.

An exchange of gunfire and a lengthy chase across the desert later, and I followed them as they pulled into a train station. Smoke rolled from the stack and I was sure that the train was prepared to leave. I wasn't certain that I could subdue them before they were aboard.

I leapt from my truck and ran inside. In the race for the title of 'Most Idiotic Idea', the decision to run blindly into the train station was at the top of the list.

As I ran through the door, a solid fist came in from the left faster than I could react. It clipped me in the jaw and I went down hard.

I'm not new to the fighting game and I came up with my

pistol drawn. As I brought it around, a hand clamped around my wrist and yanked me to my feet.

These Nazis were fast.

They punched me twice in the gut and again in the chin. I felt my brain rattle in its cage and began to wonder if these foreign thugs had decided against wasting bullets on me, instead intending to beat me to death.

As I shook my head and looked around, I realized that I was completely immobilized. At each arm one of the large Nazis held me tight. My head was being held from behind by an arm around my neck and a hand on my forehead. I was stretched out and couldn't move. The entire means through which I had been immobilized would have been impressive if I hadn't been the one they were using it on.

"Andrew Doran." A man hissed as he walked toward me from the platform. His eyes were like a snake's, literally. He was a child of Yig, the snake god, and it looked like he was a member of the Nazi army as well.

Aside from the snake eyes, he looked like your average member of the Aryan race. He had blond hair cut short on the sides and combed to the side and a military physique. He was dressed in a plain brown suit, and could have passed for a Professor at my university if he didn't have the snake-eyes.

Of course, we'd probably still hire him even with the snake-eyes.

He smiled broadly as he spoke. "Dean of Missskatonic Universsssity, Anthropologissst, and warrior for good againssst all of the monstersss that go bump in the night." His voice was a mix of a German accent with a less than subtle hiss. He was definitely his father's son. He laughed. "For a man who isss known to have ssscattered the Traum Kult to the windsss, you are not very impressssive in your current ssstate."

I smiled through a split lip that I could feel trickling blood down my chin. "You're doing it all wrong." I tried to shake my head and remembered the very strong man behind me. "First you introduce yourself, and then I knock out your men, beat you, and then take that journal."

The snake-eyed German brought up his left hand with the

leather journal. He waved it in my face. "Do you mean thisss journal?" He punched me in the stomach then and if I could have doubled over I would have. "Now, what would Dr. Andrew Doran want with the diary of the mad old William Dyer?"

I didn't have to tell him. He knew why I wanted the journal. It was a book of power, and lately I'd become a librarian. By librarian, I specifically mean that I'm always chasing books. At least that's how it felt.

The trip to Dyer's cabin had been a shot in the dark. I wasn't actually expecting to find Dyer there, but I knew that any scientist worth his degree had a journal somewhere and the cabin was the most likely of places.

I had been looking for William Dyer and his journal because he had been one of the few survivors of a doomed expedition to the Antarctic. When he'd returned to the United States he ranted and raved about a city in those frozen mountains that housed an ancient race of monsters. Whatever he found, he had managed to describe a city of ancient aliens and their technologies hidden for thousands of years on the frozen continent. My interest had piqued.

My predecessor to the position of Dean at Miskatonic University had been a traitor to his country and all of humanity. He had taken Dyer's knowledge to the Traum Kult, a Nazi Occult organization determined to use the creatures from our nightmares to rule the world. It was very likely that the knowledge that Dean Brandon Smythe took to the Nazis was that the technologies in the Antarctic could be used in the war effort. My only hope of preventing the Nazis from getting that technology was to find William Dyer and get to the Antarctic first.

Or, find his journal.

I didn't have to say any of this, and the spawn of Yig wasn't about to give me a chance to.

"My name is Olof." He took my pistol from the Nazi on my right and started eyeing it. "Sssee, I *can* be polite."

My pistol was an old .38 Smith and Wesson. It had runes carved along the barrel that gave it a certain magical ability. My gun could kill monsters that normal guns couldn't. That made it special in every sense of the word. It was *my* gun.

It bothered me that he had even touched it.

Olof slid the pistol into his belt and then looked me in the eyes. "I have now introduced myself, Dr. Doran. I believe you promisssed to knock out my men." He pointed up to the clock above the ticket master's booth and smiled. "I do not have all day."

I struggled in the grip of my captors. They only tightened their hold. "Don't make the mistake of thinking that you have any control here, Olof," I said. "You're on my clock."

Olof laughed and his Nazi thugs laughed with him. I joined in and together we killed a good thirty seconds more as we laughed together.

Olof punched me again, interrupting my laugh. I wheezed in the grasp of the bigger Nazi men and tried to speak.

"What wasss that you sssaid?" Olof asked.

I smiled at him again and this time my smile conjured fear within those snake eyes. "I said," I managed to wheeze, "that you should probably board your train."

Olof forced a smile and put his face only inches from mine. "And why would I want to do that?"

My eyes drifted past Olof. The Yig worshiper's eyes followed mine and fell on the clock above the ticket-master's station.

"Because," I answered, "I didn't come alone."

Olof looked at me, his snake eyes went wide. He looked around me and toward the door.

To my disappointment, and Olof's relief, nothing happened.

Olof's look turned to one of confusion and then he smirked, flashing teeth that looked as if they must have been filed to points.

I smirked back. "You'll have to forgive him." I said. "He's French."

Olof shrugged and turned toward the platform. "Kill the Anthropologissst," he said over his shoulder.

Suddenly, and about fifteen seconds later than we had planned, an engine could be heard revving up over the sound of the train. Olof spun on his leather Nazi boots and stared at me. I returned his stare with a genuine smile, flashing him my teeth.

The two men holding my arms relaxed as they looked over their shoulders toward where I ran into the station. As they relaxed, I pulled on my arms enough to give me the leverage to toss my head back, flattening the nose of the Nazi holding my neck. He released me to grab at his nose and I yanked my right arm free, twisting it away and to the left, tackling my third captor and kicking at the midriff of the Nazi who had been holding my right arm. We all broke up and fell away just in time.

The front of the train station exploded inward and debris battered me as I fell on the Nazi still clinging desperately to my left arm. The Nazi who had been holding my neck disappeared in a crunch under the weight of the truck that had come barreling in.

I pumped my fist into the face of the Nazi still clutching me and he fell away.

As I stood up, I saw that Olof had ran out onto the platform. Finally following my advice, the German snake-man boarded the train. The train itself was already pulling away, and I wasn't going to be fast enough to jump onto it. Turning to the truck, I reached through the driver's side window and smacked the Frenchman, Leo Dubois, on the arm.

"What took you so long?"

In heavily accented English, Leo answered by pointing at his wristwatch. "You bought the watch. Your American-made machinery is shit!"

I ignored the barb and jumped into the bed of the truck. "Go after the train!"

The Frenchman gunned the engine and the truck crashed through more of the station as it widened the path to the platform.

I had met Leo Dubois in France about a year previously. He had been instrumental in my traveling through Nazi dominated Europe. Leo had been a member of the French Resistance until I had introduced him to a world of monsters and beasts from beyond the veil of reality as we know it. He'd realized that if the Nazis were to get control of those monsters then France would be much worse off than it already was in

Nazi control. In the capacity of a soldier against the monsters, Leo had joined me in my return to America.

Leaping the platform, the truck almost threw me as Leo jerked the wheel and took us onto the tracks. It was everything I could do to stay on the truck while Leo bounced over the rails. The thud-thud-thud reverberated through my body as it tossed me about the back of the truck. I gripped the edges of the truck bed with all of my strength as I shouted, and was largely ignored, for Leo to get off the tracks.

After I was certain that I wouldn't make it much farther without being tossed out, Leo jumped the rails again and the ride smoothed out. We weren't on a road, so the ride was far from smooth, but it was manageable and versus the tracks themselves I was on a pleasure cruise.

Leo managed to keep the truck stable as he caught up to the caboose of the train. Having just left the station, the train hadn't reached maximum speed yet, but the speed was climbing and it was turning into a game of cat and mouse as Leo would catch up with the caboose and then it would start to pull away.

Finally, Leo had brought the truck along the side of the train. We were dangerously close to it, but we still were not close enough for me to grab the rail on the back of the caboose. I stretched out my hand and tried to close the gap between the truck and the train, but it was no use.

I decided then that if I was going to make it, I was going to have to jump. I steadied myself on the back of the truck and waited through two large bumps before taking two steps and jumping off the edge of the bed.

At the same time I made my move, Leo must have thought I needed a boost. He swerved the truck as I jumped and instead of having to reach out to the caboose rail, it greeted me in the abdomen, blasting the air from my lungs. I started to fall, and clutched at the railing under my arms. Pulling myself over, I glared at Leo as he pulled in behind the train.

The train was a relief compared to riding in the back of Leo's truck while we'd been on the tracks. The steady rocking of the train was as solid as the Earth itself by comparison, and

I took a moment to compose myself before slapping my hand to my holster...

...and remembered that Olof, that snake-eyed bastard, still had my pistol.

I threw open the caboose door but I did it while standing to the side. When no gunfire came exploding out, I peeked in and saw no one at all. The car was filled with a couple of small boxes and general supplies. I stepped in and saw some extra chairs stacked in a corner. This train was using the car for storage.

I ran through the car, not wasting my time there and came to the next car with less care. Stepping in, I immediately noticed that the car was stacked on each side with luggage.

The second thing that I noticed was the three Nazis standing around a makeshift table that still had a pile of cards across it. Olof must have interrupted their card game when he ran through.

While they weren't dressed as Nazis it was easy to tell that they were. The soldiers of the Nazi army, specifically those who had worked with the *Traum Kult*, all seemed to hold themselves a certain way. It was as if they thought they were better than everyone else.

They were also holding pistols aimed in my direction.

The guns began to roar from two of the closer German soldiers, but the third Nazi turned and ran from the car. I assumed that he was going to alert Olof.

Leaping out of the way, I jumped behind the stack of luggage to my right. All the luggage was stacked tightly, and as the bullets flew, I had a quick idea. Throwing my weight behind my shoulder, I slammed into the luggage and leaned. I was pushing it forward and away from the carriage wall. The tightly stacked row of luggage all moved together and fell into the cramped walkway where the Nazis were shooting.

They must have assumed that my intention had been to knock them out with the falling luggage, because they stopped firing for just a moment to laugh loudly at me. Fortunately, the thought of knocking them unconscious with the luggage hadn't even entered my mind. Instead, I used the break in the gunfire to scoop up a wide, black suitcase and push it out and in front of me.

When you use a piece of luggage as shielding, the most important thing to remember is that luggage can't stop all the bullets. If you think that, then you're dead. It'll stop some of the bullets and it might even stop most of the bullets, but you're using two pieces of wood or fabric with more fabrics squeezed between them. It's that squeezing of fabric that stops the bullet so you don't want to use a necessarily heavy suitcase so much as you want to use a solidly packed suitcase.

I could feel as I lifted the suitcase up and over my torso that I had chosen wisely. While the suitcase had weight to it, it didn't jostle around at all. It was packed very tightly.

I began walking toward them, and I did it quickly. I didn't want them to have time to realize that shooting my feet would be an easy way to end my advance.

When they stopped to load another clip into their pistols, I swung the suitcase as hard as I could into the nearest Nazi soldier. I let the suitcase fall with him and spun back at the other soldier. Before he could pull the trigger, I swatted the gun aside and slammed my fist into his face. With satisfaction, I watched as his eyes rolled back into his skull and he collapsed to the floor of the car.

I didn't waste any time on the downed soldier and instead returned my attention to the Nazi that I'd hit with the suitcase. I fell on him and hit him twice, before picking up the suitcase that I'd dropped earlier and raising it above my head.

With a grunt, I brought the case down on the Nazi's face a couple of times until he stopped moving.

Relaxing, I dropped the suitcase again and stood up. I scooped up the extra clips and both of the pistols. I checked the chamber on the pistols, put one in my waistband, and moved toward the next car.

I opened the door to the next car and stopped as I noticed all the eyes. This was a passenger car and all the passengers' eyes were on me. More importantly, they were on the dirt-covered man who had just barged into their quiet car with a pistol in the air.

A few of the women started but no one made any move to do anything other than stare at me. I frowned for a minute and remembered where I was.

This was the greatest nation in the world. The most evil things that this nation could face were currently using this train as their get-away vehicle.

"I'm looking for the Nazi bastards who just ran this way." I said, just loud enough for everyone in the car to hear clearly.

There was silence and I was beginning to wonder if maybe the whole train had been filled with Nazis when an elderly man from the other end of the car stood slowly. He grabbed the seat back that he had just risen from and swayed with the rocking of the train.

"You mean that tow-headed son of a bitch with the devil-eyes?" he shouted.

I nodded.

"He ain't in here. He moved on to the next car." The man looked proud of himself.

I ran forward until I was at the man and gave him my thanks.

"I should go with you," he added. "You might need back up."

Calling the vocal passenger an old man was being generous. He was barely able to stand with the rocking of the train and asking him to be my backup just wasn't in the cards.

I pulled the pistol from my waistband and handed it to him butt first. "I actually need you to stay here, friend. If anyone comes after me, put them down. Am I clear?"

The man took the pistol and saluted. "Captain James Sterling. Fought in the Great War. I've got practice killing Germans. You can count on me."

I saluted him back and then went on to the next car.

I wasn't worried about Captain Sterling at all. I'd left one Nazi in the last car dead and the other pretty close, but giving him the pistol would keep the passengers calm.

Of course, in my travels I'd learned that dead isn't always a permanent state. It was always good to have someone watching your back.

I slid the door open to the next car but didn't step in. As I did so, bullets flew out of the hatch and slammed into the metal door of the previous car.

I took a quick second to peek in. To my relief, the next car was filled with Nazi soldiers and no passengers. I aimed my pistol in and fired blindly, hoping to scatter them.

Not taking the time to see if it worked, I grabbed the access ladder and climbed to the top of the car. Sand and wind buffeted my face and I had to raise my arm to shield myself just to move forward. From the top of the train, I could also see Leo and the truck about three cars ahead.

I began walking forward and shooting down into the car, trying to place my bullets where I thought I had seen Nazis. It wasn't precise, but it was the only thing that I could think to do that might keep them from shooting up at me.

My suppressive fire didn't work at all. Instead, as soon as I began shooting down into the car, bullets began exploding up through the roof and toward me.

I hopped lightly, allowing the train's movement to carry me back and then rolled off the side of the carriage as the bullets continued to pop up under my feet.

Terror gripped me for a moment as my hands fumbled to find a purchase. Here I was, Monster-Hunter and Nazi-Killer, about to be killed by falling off a train. I wasn't just scared, but I was embarrassed, too.

Finally, my hands grabbed the lip of the train, and I just let instinct kick in. I allowed my weight to shift into my legs, bringing my momentum down harder than it would have been if I had just fallen, and used the tenuous grip that I had on the roof of the train to swing my legs in.

It was only by luck that I had lined up with one of the car's windows. I crashed through it and ignored the glass that sliced into my body.

There were no passengers in the car, but plenty of places for those nonexistent passengers to sit. I slammed into a seat and felt the wind go out of me. I tried to bring up my pistol, but I was too slow and a bullet hit me in the arm.

I retreated then, falling back into my chair. As soon as I

touched the seat again, I bounced back into the open. I didn't wait, I just began firing.

My first two shots were spot on and the two nearest Nazis fell without making a sound. My next shot winged one Nazi and he fell back. I turned and shot the other two Nazis, each in the head, before turning to finish off the wounded one.

My eyes searched the car quickly trying to assess if that had been all of the Germans in this car. Once I was satisfied that had been all of them, I looked at my arm.

I had been lucky. The bullet had passed straight through. I tore some cloth from one of the dead Nazis and tied it around my arm. Then I grabbed one of the machine guns they'd been using and checked the magazine.

That quickly solved the mystery of how I was able to kill five German soldiers without taking too much return fire. This Nazi had emptied his clip into trying to kill me on the roof. I was willing to bet that the others had done the same.

I slammed the clip back into the machine gun when I heard the car door toward the front of the train open up. I spun, bringing the gun up as if it were loaded, and saw the German idea of Uber-Soldat.

The Super-Soldier.

It was a bare-chested man about seven feet tall and almost four feet wide. He was bald and had so much muscle on his body that his musculature was literally tearing his skin. His army boots shook the carriage with each step that he took.

And he was dead.

His flesh carried with it the lifeless coloring of a body drained of blood. His eyes were white with the cataracts of death. He was a giant, undead, Nazi.

When I had seen his size, I hadn't flinched. I wasn't a novice to fighting, and I had tricks for taking down the big guys. Most of them involved being fast: kick out his knees, box his ears, a headlock, punches to the temple, kick to the groin, and so on. Every one of those tactics went out of the window when you were fighting one of the undead.

I wasn't a novice to fighting monsters, either. The easy attacks were to use my .38 Smith and Wesson, or my Cavalry sword, both imbued with the ability to destroy the creatures of the void. Unfortunately, my sword had been impractical to bring with me on a high speed chase across Utah, and Olof still had my pistol.

That left two options, the first of which was to destroy his head. It was the only way to stop the reanimated corpses that the Germans had become so fond of using. I had no idea how I was going to do that.

The second option wasn't on the table. I was still healing, and that meant that I couldn't use option two.

All of this went through my mind in less time than it takes to blink. I spun the emptied machine gun around in the air and caught it by its barrel. Then I ran at the beast.

He stopped stomping forward, obviously confused by me running at him. When I was within striking distance, I jumped into the air and swung the machine gun as if it were a club. My target was his right temple and I was moving fast.

Whatever powers had been used to create this animated husk had been used to amplify all of his other processes as well. With blinding speed, the monster grabbed my makeshift gun and yanked it from my hands. At the same time, he punched me in the chest with an equal amount of speed.

The wind rushed from my lungs and I was sure that I heard something crack. I don't know how much time passed before I realized that the cracking noise had been my head against the far side of the car. His blow had thrown me *across* the car.

I clutched at my chest as I laid on the floor, gasping for breath, when I felt more than heard the tell-tale sound of the beast walking toward me.

I forced myself to my feet and was surprised that I was able to actually succeed at the task. The dead Nazi liked this and smiled at me.

That told me a little something more about the magic that had created the monster. If it had just been a reanimated corpse, then the monster would have no personality. It wouldn't smile.

But if it had been a soldier who had volunteered to have its soul trapped inside of its flesh while some whacked-out wizard poured enhancement spells into it then it would smile, delight in inflicting pain, and essentially have a mind of its own.

So, I had learned that I wasn't fighting a dead guy, so much as a smart dead guy.

I squared off, deciding that I was going to at least go down swinging, and the monster continued his progression toward me. Once he came within reach, he didn't hesitate to start swinging at me.

His moves were so fast, but having a personality meant that he would be drawing on skills and patterns he'd learned while a Nazi soldier, and I have beaten hundreds of Nazi soldiers.

Recognizing the swing, I ducked it with as much speed as I could muster. I almost wasn't fast enough. The wind from the swing brushed my hair. As I ducked the swing I also stepped under it and past the dead Nazi. In one fluid motion, I put my heel into the back of the Nazi's right knee.

On a normal person that move would have dislocated his knee and dropped him to the ground. The fight would have been over. Fortunately for me, I wasn't expecting any sort of normal reaction. I succeeded in pushing the beast to his knees and then proceeded to punch the back of his head as hard as I could.

I landed blow after blow into the back of his head. My hands were starting to hurt from the damage his skull was doing to them. I tried to increase the force of my blows, but in a quick move the monster spun and slapped me in the chest. The hit was just as strong as all of his previous attacks and I found myself struggling to take a breath again.

The hit had slid me back and along the carriage. I hadn't done much damage to the monster Nazi's head, but I must have at least dazed him because he was taking about as long as I was to stand back up.

That's when she showed up.

"You're going to have to use magic." She said, and I knew she was right.

Her name was Olivia and she wasn't real. She was a fractured piece of my mind and the result of my using the magic of the void too much.

The void is the name I give for all the evil and monstrous

things that are just under the surface of the world everyone knows. The void is another dimension, or an invisible world living right alongside our own. From that world, those with the talent for it can harness the energies through words, items, or gestures of power. Wizards of old did it, and so can I.

The downside to touching the void is that it was never meant for the human mind. Every time that someone touches the void they lose a piece of their sanity. Those without the affinity for the void usually go completely insane with the briefest of contacts with it. Those with the ability to manipulate it usually last longer, but it depends on how often they use it.

My insanity had started with the complete and total invention of Olivia. I needed help getting through Nazi-controlled France, and my mind conjured a French woman with all the proper paperwork.

It took me a while to figure out that she was the scar-tissue from my magic use, but when I did I decided to stop using it and give my mind a chance to heal. I didn't know if it could heal, but I had to try.

Unfortunately, I tend to run into ridiculously complicated situations that require the use of magic and I couldn't deny how right my imaginary friend was. I wasn't going to stop the monster with my fists alone. I was going to need help.

Even though I knew what I needed to do, it was a hard thing for me to convince myself to do it. Olivia had gotten quieter and easier to ignore in the last several months and it gave me hope that I had been on the road to recovery.

The rotting hulk had started walking toward me by the time I was finally up on my knees. I focused my will into grabbing the power that was within my grasp and pushing it into my hands.

I had just started summoning my will when the undead Nazi had made it to me. He grabbed me with one of his hands wrapping around my throat and lifted me up into the air.

I kept pushing my energy into my hands until the edges of my vision began to blur. The thing could have snapped my neck at any time, but that Nazi personality was as much a crutch as it was an aid. He wanted to see the life leave my body.

The moment before I would have passed out, I swung both of my hands up and slapped the side of his throat. The energy I had collected was raw power and I poured it out of both of my hands and into his neck.

His dead eyes widened with surprise as he realized that he had miscalculated. I felt his hand begin to tense in hopes of killing me first but the undead monster wasn't fast enough. My magic tore through his flesh and in the same instant that his head fell off his shoulders, his hand released me and I fell to the ground.

For the third time in almost as many minutes, I gasped to fill my lungs with air.

Olivia was suddenly in front of me as I choked on the dry Utah air.

"Get up, we don't have time for this."

I frowned at her and then forced myself to my feet. I had no weapons and was bruised, but I didn't think either was an issue that would hold me back.

I got to the door to the junction between the cars and slid it open noisily. As soon as I had my head through it I saw a gun and dove back.

No bullets came, but a loud clunk did and I felt the car jolt underneath my feet. Whoever was in the next car had just separated the cars.

I swore and swung back out of the carriage door. I didn't wait to see if anyone was firing at me, instead choosing to bet on my speed and luck. I swung around and up the ladder on this side of the carriage as bullets bounced around me. Within moments I was back on the roof.

The wind tore at me, but not like it had before. I only had a moment to act so I took a few steps back from the edge of the roof, then turned and sprinted toward the edge.

The gap between the cars was further than I had assumed it was and I almost missed my target. I grabbed the bottom of the ladder on the other car by sheer luck. The gunman was just barely in reach and I grabbed him by the ankle and bounced him off the tracks and into the way of the slowing car.

Speed was on my side and I bounced my legs off the tracks

and swung myself onto the ladder. I continued to the roof and moved as quickly as I could toward the edge of the train. Deciding that touching the void was the only way I was going to have any chance at success, I gathered my energies and then swung down over the edge of the roof and into another window.

Unlike the first time, I was prepared for the jump. The window shattered and I hit the floor of the car with one tight roll and came up ready.

I sent a wave of pure energy at the first form I saw. To my satisfaction it was Olof, and the gun he was holding was knocked from his hand.

I didn't slow to see if Olof had gone down with the hit, instead choosing to tackle the only other occupant of the room.

The other occupant wasn't special at all. He was just another Nazi and not an undead one at that. I hit him in the abdomen with my shoulder and drove him back into the other side of the car.

I heard a window break in that moment and knew he'd hit the window hard. I stood up and reared back to punch him when I heard magical words being barked from behind me.

I spun just in time to see Olof with his palm out toward me. A wave of invisible energy, similar to what I had sent at him, hit me and almost knocked me back out of the car.

I stopped myself from sliding out the door of the car by grabbing at the floor. I came up with the gun that Olof had lost with my initial attack.

I was beyond pleased when I realized that it was my Smith & Wesson.

The Nazi I had slammed into the window swung his own gun in my direction.

He didn't understand though. I had just taken out an entire battalion of Nazis without my weapon of choice. He didn't stand a chance.

My bullet landed between his eyes, and he fell out the window that was broken behind him.

I brought my gun arm around and put Olof in my sights. I was prepared to pull the trigger when Olof hissed another magical phrase. The gun writhed as it turned into a snake and I dropped it to the carriage floor.

"That had better not be permanent." I growled.

Damned snake monsters.

Olof ran at me then, but I was no longer in the mood to fight. The undead Uber-Soldat was more than enough fighting for me.

I ducked Olof's quick swing, but I had assumed that Olof was more human then snake, and suffered for it. Humans have poor recovery when they miss unless they've had it trained out of them. Olof missed and managed to twist and strike me in the back of the head.

The floor met me with a bounce before I was picked up, spun around and hoisted, again, by my throat.

Olof had more of his father in him than I had originally surmised.

Whatever power Olof had tapped into to hold me, it was at least as strong as the undead Nazi's had been. I was immobilized and suffocating.

Olivia appeared silently behind Olof then with a smile. "Are you really going to make me save you?" She was using her French accent again. "He has defensive energies up. It's going to take all of my power." Which since Olivia was a figment of my imagination, what she really meant was that it was going to take all of *my* power.

Olivia walked slowly around Olof until she faced him just to my right side. With a quick move of her arm, she punched the snake-eyed bastard in the stomach.

Surprise and pain flashed across Olof's face as he doubled over and dropped me to the floor.

Olivia had faded from sight, but her voice was clear in my mind. "I wish I could do more, but someone has left me all tied up and without exercise for the last few weeks." There was a heavy sigh. "You're on your own now. Don't get us killed, s'il vous plait."

I didn't wait to catch my breath. Standing up quickly, I gave an uppercut to Olof. His head snapped back and Olof was immediately twisting away.

Not allowing him to gain any ground, I followed as Olof

twisted and I kicked at him. Snake or not, that area between his legs was all man. Olof howled as I grabbed the back of his head by its blond hair and put my fist into his face three times.

Letting Olof go, he fell to the ground and then jumped forward toward a snake writhing on the floor.

Then I realized it had never been a snake. Olof hadn't turned my gun into a snake, he had just managed to convince me that it was a snake.

My eyes darted around the floor as quickly as they could until I found what I was looking for. The Nazi that I had watched fall out of the car window with a bullet sized hole in his head hadn't taken his pistol with him.

Diving across the floor, I went into a slide and scooped up the Nazi pistol.

Olof brought my gun to bear on me at the same time I brought the pistol to bear on him.

We shot at the same time.

Olof's head snapped back and he fell over. The wood next to my head splintered.

My heart was beating so fast that I could feel it in my whole body. That bullet had been really close.

I dropped the Nazi gun and pried my prized pistol from Olof's dead fingers before patting down Olof.

It didn't take me long to find the journal in Olof's inside jacket pocket. I flipped through the pages, eager to find the clues I had been waiting for.

I flipped the pages faster, and with each page my heart sunk further.

The pages weren't covered in words, but in the symbols of a language that I didn't recognize. It was in code.

I sighed heavily and said to no one in particular, "I'm going to have to find William Dyer."

Chapter 2: Miskatonic University

The returning train ride to Miskatonic University was completely uneventful. I mulled over William Dyer's journal the entire journey, while Leo alternated between sleeping and drinking wine. I flipped through page after page of Dyer's ramblings. Some of it included words and sentences that almost made sense, but even those came across as what I could only assume was coded gibberish.

The runic writings filled the rest of the pages, with each page making less and less sense. I had spent most of my life researching the darker historical texts of the world, and while I recognized most of the runes, they were completely out of context. Without William Dyer, I wasn't going to ever understand that journal.

Before long, I gave in and joined Leo in the more enjoyable of his Frenchman habits. Together we finished quite a few bottles of wine before finally returning to the east coast.

Once we had returned to the University, I swung by my office for only a moment to drop off my weapons and grab a bottle of brandy before heading directly for the library.

I had only just poured myself a glass when Leo was able to join me. He collapsed into one of the more comfortable chairs and ignored the stares he received from the few students that stuck around during the summer months. I walked to where he had collapsed and handed him the glass.

"Monsieur, you have an office. Shouldn't we discuss our matters there?" Leo raised an eyebrow toward one of the students walking by and then swigged the brandy.

He had a point, of course. Our discussions weren't meant

for the curious ears of the students at Miskatonic University, but that office hadn't always been mine.

"Brandon Smythe had an office. I prefer being in the library or in the field."

I poured myself a drink and then turned and tossed the useless journal onto a pile of books that had started to collect next to Leo's chair. This had been our place of research for the last several months and I had told the librarian that each of the volumes we had collected should remain within reach. The titles that Dyer's journal landed next to were not titles that many of the students would ever need anyway. Titles such as *Deep Beneath the Granite Lies Madness*, by Dr. Alan Scott, *Precursor to Prehistory*, by Dr. Jonathan Stewart, and *The Alien Ancestors*, by Connor Hawke. While not a man of higher learning, Connor Hawke was considered one of the world's most knowledgeable resources in matters pertaining to outside of Earth's atmosphere. At least, that was the case for those who believed in such matters. Unfortunately, the world was ruled by the ignorant, and poor Mr. Hawke would never be known as much more than a crackpot.

Leo noticed the frustration in my face as I tossed Dyer's journal. "You have had no luck then?"

I shook my head at my friend. "None." I sat across from Leo in a chair similar to the one that he occupied. "Why would someone that was so ready to label himself insane in the eyes of the 'educated' world by warning the world of what he saw, hide the details of what he told us all about in such an indecipherable mess?" I was asking the question rhetorically, but Leo answered anyway.

"He obviously had much more to tell." Leo's lip curled into a half of a smile. "Are you not the master of keeping the world from knowing what it is you truly do? Does this seem so hard for you to understand?"

I frowned back at my friend, but it didn't change the fact that he had a valid point. In my quest to protect humanity from the horrors that lay just out of sight, I had hidden many truths. Not even Leo, whom I trusted more than anyone alive, knew the full extent of what our enemy could do. Instead, I told him only what he needed to know, but Leo's point was possibly closer to the truth than he knew.

I did not hold back data from Leo because of any sort of trust issues, but instead to protect him. The little bit of the void that he had already seen had almost shattered his psyche. I knew that I wouldn't be able to protect him forever, but I was in no hurry to hasten his descent into madness. By that same token, William Dyer had told the world what they needed to know. It was possible that whatever was in that journal would drive me deeper into madness.

If Olivia's resurgence was any indication, I couldn't really afford to go any crazier.

We were interrupted then by Carol Berg, my secretary.

"Dr. Doran, thank goodness you've returned," she sounded genuinely relieved to see me. Carol was in her early twenties and only a few inches shorter than myself. She wore her brown hair up in a tight bun and was an attractive woman when she smiled.

Unfortunately, I was never going to see her smile while she worked for me. I couldn't get used to the idea of having a secretary, and regularly ignored my responsibilities to my recently acquired position. While I might be the Dean of Miskatonic University, I was also in the middle of a war for the soul of humanity.

I am a man of priorities.

"Carol, please join us for a drink." I said, trying to head off the bureaucratic nonsense that I knew was coming.

Her relief at finally finding me evaporated into a very heavy frown. "I would love to, sir, but I simply do not have the time." She threw a glance at Leo before continuing. "And neither do you. I have a large collection of agreements for you to sign that are currently waiting patiently for you on your desk. Those forms are for the renovations to Pellman Hall. Underneath those, you'll find several requests for admission that still need to be approved by yourself."

I frowned. Normally, there was a department for handling admissions and the Dean would be able to excuse himself from that task. Unfortunately, I had made it quite clear that

Miskatonic University needed a more stringent vetting process. Over the years, cult enthusiasts, devil worshipers, and plainly insane people had been admitted to the University and granted access to some of its darker secrets. Under my oversight, I wasn't going to allow that to happen anymore and had fully taken over the role of filtering through our candidates.

To Carol's point, I wasn't very good at it.

"How many requests is 'several'?" I asked.

"Two hundred seventy-eight as of this morning." She replied without hesitation.

Leo laughed out loud at that and I shot him a glare.

"Carol," I said. "I will head directly to my office in just a moment. Leo and I are nearing a breakthrough in our research. I will address everything on my desk by the end of the day. You have my word."

Carol had had my word on previous occasions as well and didn't say anything as she spun on her heel and stormed out of the library.

Still smiling, Leo asked, "Should we go to your office?"

I shook my head. "Not yet. If we can't translate Dr. Dyer's journal, then they won't be able to stop the Germans from getting weapons that could destroy the world." I grinned. "Admission would be the least of our worries."

Leo leaned back in his chair and took another sip of his brandy. "We do not know that they are weapons, though. Dyer's city in the mountains could be a home to pacifists."

I shook my head and pointed at a folder resting beside my chair. "That's Dyer's edited account of the expedition. His 'warning'. If his interpretations of the carvings are correct, then their reign on this planet came to a halt during a war. Wars have weapons. The Nazis will find something."

"This is bigger than us. Maybe we should take this to the United States Government?"

I laughed at Leo's statement, even though he was probably being serious. "They would just take the weapons for themselves. Everyone that we might normally go to, in regards to stopping Nazi threats, is useless because everyone that we go to will want to use whatever weapons are down there, and we can't allow that. It is not technology for this world and the allure will be irresistible."

"Then we need to find William Dyer." Leo's grasp of the obvious did little to advance our situation. "If the Nazis don't have him already."

"They don't." I replied.

Leo wasn't about to just accept that the Nazis didn't have Dyer at my word alone, and I didn't blame him. "But, how can you be certain?"

I shrugged, "We only went looking in Utah because we couldn't find William Dyer in the usual locations. I'll bet the Germans did the same thing. As of our parting with them in Utah, the Germans don't have Dyer."

"What about Dyer's office?" Leo asked.

Leo hadn't been there when the same idea had passed through my mind. Dr. William Dyer had been a member of our Geology department at Miskatonic University. He was never released from that position, and his tenure kept him in ownership of his office even though he hadn't been there for more than a year.

I nodded. "I went to look, but it was locked up."

Leo scoffed. "Locks stopped you?"

"Locked with magical wards," I corrected. Whatever Dyer had learned when he had been in those frozen mountains, it had taught him at least how to make strong enough wards to keep out a practitioner as powerful as myself.

Leo smirked. "I did not know that doors were so formidable for the great Dr. Andrew Doran."

I glared at Leo for just a moment before making a decision. Standing, I stormed out of the library, knowing Leo would be fast on my heels.

We arrived at Dyer's office at the same time. It was a simple wooden door and, aside from the plaque with his name on it, it looked like every other office door.

Unless you could see the powers that leaked from the void into our world.

I pointed at the door and threw a glance at my companion. "Can you see them?"

The door looked to me as if symbols had been carved into the reality around the door. The wood was untouched, but the reality that was the wood had been carved into wards. Each ward was filled with the faint purple hue that my mind associated with the void. It wasn't really a color, but it was the best description of a color that could not be described.

Leo had been touched by the void enough that he should have been able to see something on the door.

He squinted at it before saying, "It has a color. Almost purple?"

I nodded. "That would be the wards." As I had feared, Dyer had learned much more than he had told in his loudly voiced warning.

Leo nodded and continued. "While I can see the wards, this changes nothing." He waved his hands about indicating where they were. "We are on the first floor. The windows should be easily accessible."

I could have slapped myself right then. In my haste to enter the room, I hadn't even thought of the windows. I pushed past Leo and headed back the way that we had come and then out of the main hall.

We circled around the building until we were right outside of Dyer's office when Leo voiced the obvious. "Someone has already broken into Dyer's office."

My righteous fury took over, and I corrected Leo. "No, they broke into my school." I nodded toward the window as I walked toward it. "Give me a lift."

Leo crouched quietly under the window and laced his fingers together in order to saddle my foot. Using my friend's lift, I peered into the shattered window.

Inside the office was a mess, and I could quickly tell that it wasn't entirely due to the actions of the vandal. William Dyer had the office of a professor and it was a clutter of books, loose papers, and more books. On the contrary, the vandal didn't even seem to be making a mess, instead putting everything back where she found it as she searched for something.

She was only a few inches shorter than myself with shoulder-length blonde hair. She wore a leather jacket and trousers, which made sense: a dress wasn't thieving wear.

I hadn't realized that Leo was no longer supporting me until I heard the click of a hammer being pulled into place. Glancing down, and hanging on the sill, I noticed that Leo had drawn a pistol from seemingly nowhere.

I nodded to the gun. "Hold back," I whispered. "I'm going in. I might need you out here."

Leo returned my nod, but said nothing. Leveraging my elbows into the window, I pulled myself in. I tried to be quiet, but it didn't matter. My quarry was so engrossed in whatever was at Dyer's desk that she wouldn't have heard if the entire school had been collapsing around her.

I slid my upper torso into the window and was drawing my leg up as she spun. I must not have been as quiet as I had hoped. She saw me and roughly threw down what she'd been examining back onto the desk.

The would-be thief knocked over a precariously leaning stack of Dr. Dyer's books, throwing debris in my path as I completed my journey into the room. She spun away from me then and toward the door.

Before I had time to warn her that the door had been warded with a slew of unknown spells, she flung the door open wide and ran from the room with absolutely no consequences.

Of course, if I were to have warded the door, I also would have only warded against intrusion, and not escape. My hindsight was in full focus.

I hurdled over the fallen stack of books and to the desk, only quickly examining what had held her attention.

It was a picture in a frame.

I didn't slow by much and scrambled from the room and down the hall. I silently cursed myself for not alerting Leo, and I hoped that he had caught on and was circling around to the front of the building.

The halls in the University were tight, so both of our speeds were slowed by the back and forth traffic moving through them. Two more bookshelves, for public reference, were hurdled into my path before she cleared the hall and exited the building.

Jumping over both fallen shelves, I called back to the nearest young student, "Bonus credit for cleaning this mess!"

Leo met me at the front steps with his right hand inside his jacket. I glanced at the crowd that surrounded us and then down the street, before shaking my head at Leo. We couldn't use guns here. Our culprit was heading for an empty car and there were way too many students between us and her.

I renewed my charge after her as she slid into the car and took off, her tires squealing as they spun on the road. This time, though, my target wasn't the woman who had fled Dr. Dyer's office, but instead the motorcycle that was parked right out front as if it had been prepared especially for me.

Of course, the student who was standing beside it didn't think so. I offered him a 4.0 for the semester and then took off on his shiny 1941 Crocker.

The Crocker was the perfect blend of solid craftsmanship and organic design. The colors were a splattering of black around the fenders and seat and then chrome everywhere else. The curves to the machine reminded me of some sort of elegant sea creature. I had never been much into motorcycles, but this bike could easily change my views.

I weaved the bike between the oncoming traffic and pedestrians. Sidewalks and lanes didn't matter to me. I hopped the curb and gunned the engine as I found an open stretch of sidewalk. It helped me to close the distance and I hopped the curb again and came up directly behind the trespasser.

Without a doubt, the roar of the motorcycle warned my quarry to my presence. Against my assumption, she didn't speed up. Instead, with me close on her tail, she stomped heavily on the brakes.

The car screeched to a halt, sliding a little bit as it did. Only my fast reactions saved me from the surprise maneuver. I leaned to the left and hit my brakes as well. I only narrowly slid past her on the driver's side of the car and was too busy righting myself to notice as she then put the car back into gear and took off.

Once I had the Crocker back under my control, I looked behind me just in time for my target to zoom past me. As she did so, she opened her door and hit me with it.

My balance was destroyed and I went sprawling with the bike onto the roadway. Together, the beautiful machine and I slid for about twenty feet before I was able to get it back up and down the road again.

I went into this race assuming that her age placed her in the novice weight class in regards to car chases. I wasn't going to make that mistake again. I had been in more car chases, wrecks, and fights than she had, of that I was sure.

The Crocker roared down the street with me leaning forward and into the wind. I closed the distance to my quarry again, and this time I decided to test her. I pulled up right next to her window and reached out for her. I wasn't actually trying to grab her, but I wanted her to think that I was.

My trick worked and the would-be thief swerved to the right slightly to avoid my grasp. Her reaction told me two very useful things.

The first of which, I had already begun to suspect: she wasn't German. If she had been working for the Nazis she would have pulled a gun and gotten rid of me already. No, she just wanted me to leave her alone.

The second thing that her reaction told me was that, despite her clever move with the brakes previously, she was a novice to car chases. This wasn't only new to her, it was foreign to her. She wasn't a professional crook.

Betting on my hunches, I sped up and advanced just ahead of her front left tire. Being that much in front of her, she couldn't tell what I was doing when I lifted my arm, reached across my chest, and then quickly swung my arm back and took aim at her face.

My index finger had never been registered as a lethal weapon, but the criminal mastermind behind me didn't take the time to evaluate the caliber of my weapon.

The novice thief swerved to avoid my imaginary pistol, exactly as I assumed she would. Doing so had the intended result of putting her car directly into the path of a brick wall.

The crunch of the car hitting the wall drowned out the sound of the roaring motorcycle.

I parked the bike and ran back to the car to check on the

driver. She was moaning and blood was dripping down her forehead.

"Are you alright? Can you hear me?" I shouted to her. Her attention suddenly snapped back to the here and now and her eyes darted to my face. Before she could say anything, I punched her in the temple, knocking her out cold.

It probably wasn't the most intelligent thing to do, but I wasn't going to let her try to run again. As the crowds gathered around, I dragged her from the wrecked car and flopped her over the handlebars of the bike. I mumbled to the gathering spectators something about taking her to the hospital and then revved the engine toward Miskatonic.

"This," Leo stated dryly, "is when you choose to use your office?"

I ignored Leo and his slight smirk and instead studied our prisoner.

She was still unconscious, but I wasn't certain whether or not she was faking it. I hadn't hit her hard enough to keep her out that long, but the car accident might have jostled her brain, so I was unsure.

Once I had pulled the Crocker up to the school, Leo, who had been awaiting my return, helped me carry her up to the office. Once there, we threw her down on the nearest chair and began tying her to it as tightly as we could.

Looking at her for really the first time without anything else going on, I did not recognize her at all. She had short blonde hair that went only a little past her jaw line. Her eyes were hazel and her face carried a youthful quality to it. She wasn't older than her early twenties at best, but she would also keep that youthful look for a long time.

Without warning, the phantom from the shadows of my mind, Olivia, sprung into existence directly beside my captive.

"Just take the information from her mind." She pressed. "You know that you can do it without hurting her."

"No," I responded with heat in my voice, both at the intrusion of my would-be imaginary friend and at the suggestion.

Leo snapped from his own examination of our trussed up

thief with surprise. "No?" He asked. "No what?"

Much to his chagrin, I continued to ignore Leo. Olivia wasn't giving up. "We can't afford any delays. Reach into her mind and find out what she knows and why she's here." Olivia paused then, realizing that I wasn't going to reply to her and then lifted her own phantom hand. "Or I can do it..." Olivia had been born from the insanity induced through channeling the powers of the void through my brain. Because of those pathways, she was capable of doing anything with magic that I was.

Olivia reached for our guest's head with her hand and I shot her a glare.

"No," I growled at Olivia, and immediately was rewarded with Olivia sliding away from the thief as if she was being pushed by an unseen force.

I smiled inwardly, proud of myself for still having at least that little bit of control over my sanity. Pushed by an unseen force was exactly what happened, and the unseen force was me.

"She is here, no?" Leo asked, obviously referencing Olivia. I nodded and he frowned, uncomfortable by her invisible presence.

Olivia crossed her arms and frowned at me. "If you won't take what you need, then at least tell me why not."

Not caring that Leo was only going to get half of the conversation, I answered Olivia. "For starters, reaching into her mind isn't as safe as you would have me believe." I paused and sighed heavily. "And I don't think that our little trespasser here is a bad guy."

"Or gal," Olivia replied and I nodded absently and then turned my heated gaze to meet Olivia's.

"You already knew she wasn't necessarily evil, though, because I did."

Leo ignored my accusation toward Olivia and asked me, "If she is not a villain, then who is she?"

I knelt in front of our captive and leaned in close, looking closely at her face. "When I found her in Dyer's office, she was looking at a framed photograph. It was of Dyer with a young girl." I nodded toward the girl only inches from me. "I think this is here." Leaning in just a little closer, I asked, "You're his daughter, aren't you?"

With her eyes still closed, she produced a tight-lipped smile. "You're good." She opened her eyes and her face took on a smug look. "But you're only half right. I'm his estranged daughter." She put an emphasis on the word estranged.

I straightened up and looked down at her, jabbing my index finger in her direction. "Stop talking."

She jumped, as did Leo and Olivia, although Olivia did so mockingly.

"Whether or not you're Dyer's daughter doesn't really matter, because it doesn't change the fact that you were caught breaking into my college." I hadn't realized how territorial I was becoming until that moment. "For reasons that I hope you never discover," I continued, "that was ridiculously stupid."

Leo was nodding and I had to hide a smile.

Regaining my composure, I continued, putting strength behind my voice. "This is how we are going play this game: I am going to ask you questions..."

Leo coughed loudly.

"...and so will my friend." I pointed again at her. "You will answer them. The more questions that you answer truthfully, the more trust we will be able to put in you." I softened my voice. "If we trust you, we don't have to call the police."

The bound blonde scoffed at us. "Police? That's your threat?" She laughed again. "The police are the last thing that I'm worried about."

I gave no ground. "Do you see?" I pointed out. "That is a great start. I believe you." I walked across the office and grabbed a chair. I carried it over to where I had been standing and set it down in front of her.

I sat down. "Let's start simple: Who are you?"

Her mouth drew into a tight line and for a moment I thought that she wasn't going to be cooperative. Then she relaxed and said, "My name is Nancy Dyer."

I nodded. "Nancy, why were you breaking into my college?"

Nancy leaned against her ropes, bringing her face closer to mine. "Fair is fair. Why did you break into my cabin?"

I froze for a moment, and the smile that flashed across her face showed me that she noticed my hesitance. "We didn't. We chased the ones who did."

"That isn't an answer." She countered.

She was right, so I answered her. "We were looking for your father."

Nancy leaned back and lost her smile. "So was I." She looked at Leo and then back at me. "If you weren't the guys who trashed my father's cabin, then who was?"

"We'll get to that." Was the only answer that I was willing to give her, and she seemed to accept it for the moment.

"Why are you looking for your father?" Leo asked, and it was a good question.

Nancy glared at Leo, and I could tell he was happy that we had decided to tie her up. "He is my father and he is missing. I don't need a reason."

"If that were the case," I pressed, "you would have met with the campus Dean or gotten the police involved."

It was a test and I was filled with a sick satisfaction as Nancy failed it.

"Well, the Dean was supposed to meet me to let me into my father's office." She looked from me to Leo. "When the Dean didn't show for our meeting, I got tired of waiting and took the initiative."

Leo laughed loud and hard. It was a hearty laugh that filled the entire office and after several seconds of his laughter I joined in. We laughed for another fifteen to twenty seconds before Leo said, "If you were supposed to meet with the Dean, then why did you run as soon as he climbed through the window?"

Nancy's rage drained and her face paled as her eyes registered understanding.

"Oh." Was all that she could bring herself to say.

I gave a little bow while remaining seated. "Dean Andrew Doran of Miskatonic University. It is a pleasure to meet you, Nancy Dyer."

I leaned forward in my chair and folded my hands. "I'm going to be generous," I said. "I'm going to put our cards on the table." Nancy didn't look like she believed a word that I said, and she probably expected the next words that I said to be a lie, but I didn't care.

"We're interested in your father's Antarctic expedition. Unlike the rest of the world, I am willing to bet that you know a little bit more than anyone else about what actually happened to your father."

I was watching Nancy for any sort of tell. She gave no sign that she agreed with or disagreed with what I had just assumed about her.

"Unfortunately," I continued, "your father wasn't quiet about what he found and now the entire German army is interested in conducting their own expedition." I sighed. "Contrary to American hopes and dreams, the Germans aren't stupid. They know that your father wasn't spinning tales. They know that what he was warning the world about was most likely true, and they aren't about to rush to Antarctica unprepared."

Nancy's face paled, but she made no conscious reaction.

"They're after your father and they want him to take them there. As an American," Leo coughed loudly, "and a Frenchie, we don't want them to go on this expedition at all. Since we can't stop an entire army, we're trying to find your father first and offer him the best protection that we can provide."

Nancy laughed at me then. "What kind of protection could you possibly provide?"

I ignored her and smiled curtly. "Whether the Nazis find your father or not, they will go on their trip and they will find what your father did. Except they will do so with nefarious plans and try to bring it back here and use it in their war effort." I leaned back in my chair. "Instead of allowing that to happen, Leo and I also want your father for another reason. We need him to take us to those horrible mountains so that we can destroy the lost city before the Nazis can loot it."

Nancy's earlier comment on protection must have been forgotten, because she suddenly came to a realization. "Wait. Do you actually believe my father's story of the mountains?" She sounded slightly hopeful.

Leo nodded to her and answered. "We do."

I did my best not to laugh then, but it was very humorous to me. Nancy Dyer found it a daunting idea that I would believe the ramblings of her father. If she only knew of the things that I believed in.

Leo wasn't in the mood for any more revealing, and we had more or less reached the end of our information anyway.

Aside from the news about the journal.

"No more lies." Leo said it sternly, but with calm. "You know where we stand and what we want to do. Why did you break into your father's office?"

Her lips were tight while Nancy looked between Leo and myself as she wrestled with whether or not she should trust us.

In the end, she chose to trust.

"I was just a little girl when my father came back from Antarctica," she started quietly. "At first, he didn't talk about it, or much of anything for that matter. I think he just wanted to forget that it had happened at all. When he wasn't drinking at home, he would spend all of his time here, at his office and still drinking. He wasn't someone who normally preferred the bottle. He was just in a lot of pain.

"When he wasn't in his office, he would be at our cabin. When he went there it would be for months at a time. Mother and I had no idea what had happened to him, but we could see that he'd changed. We found out when the rest of the world did. When that second expedition was announced, father found his next mission: he had to stop it."

I nodded and remembered when I had first read the warning from Dr. Dyer. He had only sent it to the head of the new expedition, but upon being ignored by the expedition head, and then each of his funding sources, Dr. Dyer then publicly presented his story in hopes of being taken seriously. There were very few of us who did.

Nancy continued.

"My mother was mortified. She took immediate action to separate him from our lives. I didn't blame her, but I had looked into my father's eyes. He wasn't crazy, only scared. I believed him. She moved us to Washington D.C. and we left my father here, in Arkham. The only part of him that I could smuggle with me was a copy of his recounting of events. It was months before mother caught me reading it and took it away from me, but it didn't matter anymore. I had memorized every detail that my father had written down." Nancy twisted in her bonds. "The rest of my childhood was average and mostly fatherless. I heard less and less from him as time went by. I wanted to move to Miskatonic University to be closer to him, but my application kept getting rejected. I didn't know why, but I feel like he was trying to protect me from something."

Leo snickered, obviously thinking of all the locked doors in the University. I shot him a quick glare and he stopped.

Nancy didn't even seem to notice and continued. "I wound up at the University of Chicago, where I am currently majoring in geology. As a woman, it's already difficult being taken seriously at University, but my gender means nothing when people hear my name." She frowned. "I keep to myself mostly, at least until last week. I live in off-campus housing, alone." Anger flashed across Nancy's face. "Last week, I came home and my room had been torn apart. I had saved all of my father's letters that my mother hadn't found, and I had photographs and a collection of books that my father had published papers in. All of them had been either taken or tossed. It was obvious that they were looking for my father or something about him. I packed a few things and rushed to Utah to find my father. He wasn't there, so I changed direction and headed straight to his home in Arkham."

I had seen Dyer's house, as well. It had been worse than the cabin.

"I began to panic when I saw what they'd done to his home. That was when I came to his office. I wouldn't have had to break in if the door hadn't been covered in those heavy locks." Nancy turned her eyes to me and they were suddenly filled with anger. "If you're the Dean, how can an employee of yours disappear for months without you taking action?"

I opened my mouth to reply, but of course, Leo beat me to it.

"He is not good at his job."

I raised my eyebrow at Leo, but I didn't deny his point. "Unlike other Universities, the role of Dean at Miskatonic consists more of protecting the school instead of one of management." It was an intense understatement, but it was enough. "It keeps me very busy."

Nancy twisted in the chair again. "Now that we've got the pleasantries out of the way, how about untying me?"

Seemingly from nowhere, Olivia said, "Don't do it. She can't be trusted."

An idea came to me in that moment. Nancy had studied all of her father's work and had memorized the story that her father told. "Do you think that you could translate your father's journal if we had it?"

"Translate?" Nancy asked. "What language is it in?"

I shook my head. "Not a language; it's in code."

Nancy looked confused. "I don't know. I would have to see it." She was frowning. "I was unaware of any interest in codes that my father might have had."

"Useless." Olivia scoffed.

I continued to ignore my imaginary companion. "Nancy, we are trying to find your father to provide him with protection and save the world from what it was that he found. The Nazis will use him and then kill him when he is no longer useful. How about we help each other in the search for Professor Dyer?" I was pushing the envelope with my plea, but if she didn't understand how desperately we needed her help and the help of her father, then all was lost.

Nancy lowered her head in contemplation. My impatience grew, and I began to wonder if Olivia's warnings had been something that I should heed.

"Full disclosure." Nancy finally responded.

"What?" I asked.

"I will help you, but not without an agreement of full disclosure from both sides. Any questions you have of me, I will answer. Any questions that I have for either of you, you will also answer. Agree to that and you will have my support."

The young lady had no idea what kind of knowledge I had, but I could guess where the questions would lead.

I studied her closely.

She could take it. Nancy Dyer wouldn't balk at the answers I gave to her questions because she knew how to read people.

She had seen the truth in her father's eyes. He wasn't crazy, only scared. When I answered her questions, she would see the truth in my eyes as well, and she would not run.

I answered carefully. "I know some very dark things. Some of them could threaten your very life just by knowing them."

"That is not your decision to make. If I ask a question, I want an answer, or I walk. Right here, and right now, I tell you that no matter how dangerous to me your answer might be, I demand you give them to me." Nancy didn't say it with any sort of anger or malice. Instead, her voice was filled with the calm assurance of closing a deal.

Olivia was suddenly next to my ear. I could feel her breath on my neck as she said, "Tell her, Andrew. Tell her about what happened in the sewers to that poor model of Mr. Pickman's. Tell her that her father's psyche was most likely shattered on his expedition and that he might have begun a metamorphosis. Tell her that he might, very likely be something less … no, something more … than human. Go on, Andrew. Show her what lies beyond the curtain. Tell her. She wants to know."

I didn't say it, but she heard me think, "Only if she asks."

"Agreed," was what I said.

Nancy smiled and I thought I heard a sigh come from Leo.

I walked around to the back of the chair and began untying her bonds. Once free, Nancy began rubbing her wrists where the ropes had been.

"Where do we start?" She asked and looked expectantly at me.

I looked to Leo and he pulled out the worn journal of William Dyer.

"You do have it!" Nancy exclaimed.

Leo tossed the worn tome to its respective heir.

I nodded to her after she caught it and looked up to me, as if holding some holy relic. "Now start translating it."

Leo looked to me, and slowly Nancy's eyes pulled from the tome and followed Leo's. "And where will you be?" Leo asked me.

I smiled. "I'll be taking a nap."

Chapter 3: The Dream Lands

I had meant it when I told Leo and Nancy that I was going to take a nap, but I had also severely understated it. In all reality, I was going to use my nap to search for William Dyer.

I left them in the library and made my way back to the office as quickly as I could. Once I arrived, I closed the door and locked it behind me. I walked over to the bar and grabbed another bottle of brandy. The previous Dean's collection of brandy was impressive and with Leo and me around, I was doubly impressed by how long it had lasted. I didn't waste any time with a glass and instead took long pulls from the bottle. This needed to be a deep nap.

I took another pull and closed my eyes, enjoying the smooth burn in the back of my throat. As the last lingering taste of the brandy disappeared from my throat, I opened my eyes and said, "Come out, come out, wherever you are."

There was an audible rustle at my desk and, for the first time since I entered the room, I noticed that my chair was spun away from me, facing the window behind the desk. With a slow rotation, the chair spun and faced forward, revealing my consistent hallucination, Olivia.

Her dark hair was tied back in a bun and she was wearing a button-up top with the sleeves rolled up. She looked ready for an excavation in Egypt. A smirk was on her face, as if she knew exactly what I was about to ask of her.

She probably did.

"You called?" she teased.

I ignored her and took another pull from the brandy bottle. I replaced the glass stopper as the burn subsided in my throat. I was starting to feel the pleasant effects of the elixir.

"Yes, I called you." I finally answered her. "I'm going to the Dream Lands. Want to come?"

The Dream Lands were a place that I had only visited rarely, and less so as I've gotten older. The Dream Lands are a parallel plane of existence that lies close to ours in an interdimensional sense. It's a place where the laws of our reality hold no sway. It is so called the Dream Lands by our reality because of the easiest means through which humans can enter that reality. Inside every dream that humans have is a secret path to the Dream Lands.

The appeal of the Dream Lands is obvious to those who go there. You can stay and never age, earning yourself an immortality in that reality while in our reality your shell of a body dies. Of course, once your body does die in our reality, you become stuck in the Dream Lands with no conventional means of leaving. For some, that's ideal. Nothing appeals more to some than immortality in a magical realm. Unfortunately, that immortality is only related to aging. Your conscious avatar could still be attacked or have an accident. Injuries and death are still possible, but some see that as a preferable world.

Sleep isn't the only means to enter the Dream Lands, but it is the easiest that any normal person can access. Those who know how to look can find the doorway between worlds with ease, but most need help. That's why I called out to Olivia. The landscapes in the Dream Lands are forever changing with the wills of the people who live there. Some are forever constant, but you never know for certain where you'll end up or what circumstances you might be thrown into. Fortunately for me, I'm probably the only person in existence who doesn't have to enter the Dream Lands alone.

Olivia wouldn't just succeed as a guide, but also as my defense. She's a being of power, specifically mine, but she understood my magic in a way that I only understand it subconsciously. With beasts, monsters, nightmare creatures, and missing or dead people from all over history roaming the landscape of the Dream Lands, Olivia's power would help to keep me safe. Most importantly, she'd be an equal match if we ran into a Child of Dreams.

When people leave our world to live in the Dream Lands, they sometimes fall in love, or lust, and children are born of those unions. These children may look like us, but they are often born with gifts as unique as the world to which they were born. Olivia would be a contender for that.

I hope.

Of course, that's if Olivia agreed to come with me.

"Why this sudden interest in my help? You've ignored all of my other advice." She raised an eyebrow.

"It isn't sudden interest," I replied, slightly annoyed. "All of my … animosity toward you has nothing to do with you specifically, so much as what you represent. You're a symptom of my going insane and sometimes that makes me grumpy." I crossed over to my desk and stood across from Olivia. "My attitude doesn't blind me to your value. In this reality, you and I are one person, but I'm willing to bet that in the Dream Lands we'll be separate entities. As much as I would prefer to bring our trigger-happy Frenchman with me, it isn't possible." I sigh. "So, I'm asking you if you want to actually provide physical help to me in this search for Dyer."

It was obvious that she was excited by the idea, but Olivia has never been one to just answer without toying with me. She frowned at me, pretending to toss the idea around and weigh the pros and cons.

I know how bored she gets being trapped in my head with only minimal interaction with the world. I was offering her a day off her leash.

A smile spread across her face. "You're such a charmer. I would love to go."

Olivia stood from my chair and then waved at it dramatically, as if presenting it like a stage magician. I stepped around her and sat down.

"Is there anything that I need to do?" My words came out slower as the brandy mixed with my earlier libations.

Olivia shook her head. "Just fall asleep. Once you're dreaming, I will find you and lead you to the Dream Lands."

I nodded. It seemed simple enough. All that I had to do was fall asleep.

I folded my arms and laid my head across them on the desk. It was nap time.

It didn't take long before I opened my eyes on an all-too-familiar beach. The sand was colorless and the skies were dark. It was a beach covered with hills. The water had pushed the sands into heaping mounds and I couldn't see anything of the scenery beyond the tallest dunes.

This wasn't just the beach of my nightmares, it was the beach of my future.

That's what I've been told, anyway.

The first time that I'd seen the beach, it had been with my consciousness projected to the actual moment. In that first vision I had simply appeared and the first thing that I noticed was the...

I looked down at my feet, and there they were. Slimy, amorphous masses climbing from the brackish water. They covered the beach, creatures of every different type of shape or size but unlike anything that any human eye had ever fallen on before. These things were fluid beasts, flowing from the ocean, but temporarily taking different forms as they continued further onto the beach.

...and toward the real nightmare.

At the crest of the hill, where the creatures congregated, stood a man.

It was me.

It was prophesied that I would turn on humanity and that I would become the Bringer of Cthulhu. In that previous visit to this premonition, I fought the evil version of myself. I like to call him Dark-Doran as it helps me keep him straight in my head.

I ran at Dark-Doran, just as I had that first time. I skipped over the slimy creatures as they reached out to grab me. As they reached forward to greet him. As I got closer and closer, running and slipping in the beach sand, Dark-Doran took no notice of my approach. My doppelganger flipped open that dreaded book, the Necronomicon, and began chanting the words from the forbidden text. He was calling to Cthulhu.

That book had been destroyed. I knew that in the back of my mind. If it was the book that I thought it was, it had been destroyed by me when I had gone toe to toe with the Traum Kult. Somehow, this evil version of myself still had the book and I had to stop him.

I was moving at a good speed as I went up the hill, but it didn't matter. I was only ten feet from Dark-Doran when I slammed into an invisible barrier.

I fell back, but was on my feet again quicker than I could follow. I slapped my hands and fists against the barrier and screamed to get his attention, but I was nonexistent to him.

As my voice began to tire, a hand grabbed my shoulder and spun me around.

I came around and let a fist fly at my new attacker, but I only hit the air. Surprise filled me. Whoever I had swung at was faster than I could punch. My surprise only continue to grow when I saw who had grabbed me.

It was Olivia. She had never been part of this vision before. How did she find me? Was she part of this evil thing that had happened to me?

Suddenly, my mind was flooded with awareness. Dreams have a habit of making you forget about reality. That is, until reality forces its way back in, the way Olivia had to my dream.

Out of courtesy, or simply her own confusion, Olivia gives me a minute to catch my bearings and recall everything. Finally, when my mind had finally caught up with the situation, Olivia nodded toward the sea.

"The path to the Dream Lands is this way." She took my hand, which struck me as very odd. It was a gentle thing, and she and I had always been at odds. It was as though she feared changing my mind about letting her off her leash. Holding my hand, she led me over and past the squirming monstrosities that crawled from the brackish water. It wasn't until we were almost to the vile liquid that I realized she didn't intend to stop at the end of the shore.

Olivia sensed my sudden hesitation and spoke without looking at me. "This is the way. You're safe with me here."

The ocean was warm with a heat that radiated from deeper than man was ever intended to go. It was a heat from the center of the world, aroused by the machinations of a waking beast.

Trusting in my guide, I allowed Olivia to guide me further into that oily soup. The water climbed over my ankles and then my knees. It wasn't more than two steps and it had climbed to my chest.

Trust or not, I couldn't stop myself from closing my eyes and holding my breath as my head was encompassed by the disgusting water.

The very top of my head hadn't been submerged for more than a moment before I was suddenly under the impression that I was being painfully squeezed. It felt as though my skin had suddenly become too small for my body, and the feeling was only getting worse. In a few moments I'd be broken and crushed; a fleshy bag of fluid.

As quickly as the crushing feeling hit, I was suddenly free of it. Before I knew what I was doing, I opened my eyes and gasped for air.

I shouldn't have been as surprised as I was when my lungs actually filled with oxygen and not oily black water. Somehow, I was on dry land with dry clothes, without any water in sight at all.

I stood, grateful to be free of that oppressive force, and spun around, taking in the view. I was in a large field of blue grass. It wasn't just a slightly blue shade of green, it was sky blue and bordering on turquoise. Aside from the grass and Olivia only a few feet from me, I couldn't see any other defining characteristics of where we'd 'landed.'

Olivia had done it. She had brought me to the Dream Lands.

"Lose the surprised look before I slap it off," she said with a smirk. "This was just as important to me as it was to you."

I waved my hand at the blue grass. "A chance to frolic?"

Olivia nodded, "As well as a chance to help you. Helping you is essentially helping myself." She smiled at me and said in French, "We work better when we work together."

I hated it when Olivia reminded me of her part in the largest self-delusion of my life, but I wasn't about to let my annoyance with her poking and prodding me ruin the alliance we had formed. I ignored the remark and began walking through the field.

Maybe my anger wasn't fueled by her entirely anyway. I still had the residual pains in my mind from that nightmare version of myself I had been faced with before Olivia had come to my rescue.

"Where are you going?" Olivia jogged to catch up with me. I pointed ahead of me. "That way."

I didn't have to look at Olivia to know that she was rolling her eyes.

"I see that. Why are you going that way? You don't even know where we are."

She had a great point, but I had a pretty strong counterpoint. "Neither of us do." I pointed again, this time more specifically. "That is smoke." She noticed it for the first time. "Smoke means fire, and fire means people."

Olivia ran ahead of me and shook her head. "No. Smoke means fire in your world. Fire means people in your world. This is not your world. This is a world of beasts and realities that don't exist. Here smoke could mean a river, and a river could be a vast sea filled with creatures that live to torture idiots who believe that smoke means fire."

I didn't slow my stride and pushed past her. "Either way, it's the only option we have. Don't tell me why my ideas are wrong, tell me better ideas."

That seemed to shut her up, and I silently enjoyed it. I didn't mean for it to sound so harsh, but she knew that I was right. There was no sign of anything in any direction other than the smoke. We could either walk blindly in any direction, or hope that the smoke meant what I thought it meant.

Nazis, zombies, wizards, and beasts be damned, I was still a man of hope.

A smile crept across my lips as a small cabin crested into sight. It was almost childish how much I was enjoying Olivia being wrong, but that realization didn't change how I felt.

The cabin was directly from a fairy tale. It was slatted wood with several small and round windows. The roof was made of thatch and climbed to a very steep peak.

Without meaning to, Olivia and I both sped up as we approached the cabin. We were practically at a sprint when we finally reached the large door. It looked like it had been cut from one piece of wood. I knocked loudly and the resounding thuds of my knuckles against the wood confirmed that it was a very heavy door.

The door swung open so easily that I was startled by it. I stepped back and almost didn't see the small boy standing in front of me. He had bright blond hair and rosy red cheeks. He didn't belong in the Dream Lands, he belonged in a magazine advertisement for school supplies or milk.

"What were you doing in my field?" He demanded. His voice didn't match his features at all. His voice was deep and hoarse. It was the voice of a very old man.

That was when I remembered the most important thing to never forget in the Dream Lands: Nothing and No one are what they seem.

This boy was anything but. He was an ancient soul who had chosen to present himself as a child. The desired effect was to be underestimated, and it worked.

The other surprise that faced me, was the boy's language. The Dream Lands are filled with people from every century and location in more than our own Universe. The chances of us speaking the same language were astronomical.

It only took a moment for me to get over that second surprise. This was the Dream Lands, and the Dream Lands were a world dominated by the mind and spirit. All languages were the same, because everyone who traversed the Dream Lands spoke in the language of thoughts.

I was going to be constantly surprised if I didn't adapt soon to this new world.

I looked closer at this "boy" and could see that his eyes weren't hiding his age. Inside that shell of a child was something very ancient.

Before I could answer his question, the ancient boy stated, "She is not as she seems."

I nodded, because lying to our first encounter in the Dream Lands seemed the wrong direction to go. "I know," I replied.

The ancient boy looked from myself to Olivia before returning his gaze to me and nodding and waving us into his home. I didn't get much of a look around the tiny, and incredibly dark, space before he spoke.

"What can I do for you?" He asked. It was a simple question, and the only logical question he could have asked, but I still felt that there was a double meaning behind it.

I decided that it was Olivia's job as my guide to lead the conversation and stepped back while she spoke.

Olivia fell into her role easily. "We seek the whereabouts of a man in the waking world."

The ancient boy nodded again, slower this time. "You arrived on the outside of the Enchanted Wood. Many show up here." He looked past us and to the colored field. While in the field I couldn't see an end to it, only more field, but now I was able to see clear across it and to the dark and thick woods that were on the far side of it.

I tried to hide my renewed surprise. I was beginning to look like some poor farm kid who just got to the big city. I was looking like a tourist. That was going to get me killed.

"I can help you with your answers. I know where you can find them," he hesitated, "but nothing comes for free."

He looked away from the distant field to Olivia, and then slowly brought his eyes to me. "It will cost you a spell."

That look confirmed for me much of what I had already been thinking. Not only did this ancient boy know that Olivia wasn't what she presented herself as, but also that I was the mortal partner in our duo. He knew that I carried the knowledge of spells. It left me wondering how much more he knew or was capable of surmising.

Seemingly from nowhere, the ancient boy was chewing on something. It looked like the end of a stick of wheat, as if he were channeling his inner Mark Twain. I doubted it, though. The nature of this world meant that it could be anything, and I was betting that it was some sort of self-defense if I chose to decline his price.

I frowned at him. I'd haggled in a thousand different marketplaces for a thousand different things, and while the ancient boy was probably the most dangerous being I had ever haggled with, it didn't stop me from noticing him for the swindler he was. It was a perfect scam, as well. He was housed on the edge of what he knew to be a regular entrance to a place that everyone travels to when in the most desperate of needs.

Swindler or not, I was at his mercy unless Olivia had a better idea, and she hadn't spoken up yet.

Raising an eyebrow, I asked, "Do you have a particular spell in mind?"

An eerie smile that stretched just a little too wide, crawled onto his face. "I believe that you know which spell I might be interested in." He spoke around the straw. "There's only one spell that could be useful to one of both worlds such as myself. You learned it during your time with the Night Watchers."

Almost a year previously, I had infiltrated a dark sect of cultists that call themselves the Night Watchers. They worship the Dream Lands, and specifically the Night Gaunts who haunt the pathways between day and night. Night Gaunts have been known to steal away with the spirits of people and deposit them into the Dream Lands and are the only creatures that can easily traverse both realms.

Night Gaunts are faceless creatures, shaped mostly like people, but with the tight dark skin of a naked rat, and the vein covered wings of a bat. They are terrifying creatures with feet that can grab the spirit of a person and tear them from the reality they know before dropping them, scared and alone, in the Dream Lands.

My time with the Night Watchers was an ill-planned attempt to tear them down from the inside. I spent a long time earning their trust, but they fooled me into thinking that I had succeeded. Once they had grown tired of the entertainment of their failed infiltrator, they tied me up in the desert to suffer and die. I only didn't by the intervention of the previous Dean of Miskatonic.

I also hadn't advertised this fact to anyone, yet this ancient boy hadn't only known I had lived through it, but also that I had learned a few tricks while I was there.

"What could you possibly want that for?" I demanded.

That eerie smile of his only grew worse. "You're not that dense, Dr. Doran." When he saw that I wasn't surprised by his knowing my name, his smile dimmed. "Do you know what I am?"

I nodded. "An old soul. You reside here instead of dying with your physical body."

"I miss the real world. Your spell can give it back to me."

Anger surged through me. "At what cost?" I demanded. "You would need a body!" I was raising my voice. "I don't even know who or what you are." I crossed my arms. "It's too dangerous."

The ancient boy sighed and looked to Olivia. "Is he always so ridiculous?"

Olivia laughed, but said nothing.

"If that is how you feel," the ancient boy continued, "then leave." As he said the last word, my feet came out from under me and I was thrown through the doorway of the house by an invisible force. Olivia came running after me as I landed. The ancient boy stood in the doorway of his house. "Good luck finding what you're looking for elsewhere." He looked to the left and right of his house exaggeratedly. "Wherever that may be."

I was on my feet in a second, but I made no move in either direction. Time was different in the Dream Lands, and the longer we stayed the more likely my body was to experience some sort of failure. We needed answers in the quickest and safest way possible, but safe wouldn't guarantee any sort of results.

If it was a less dangerous spell that that ancient child was asking for, I would give it to him without hesitation. That wasn't the case. He wanted the Song of the Gaunts, and there was only one purpose for it.

Asking Olivia along with me on my journey to the Dream Lands wasn't just because I needed a guide. I also needed a safe and relatively simple way of getting there. Having her there to show me the path from my dream to the Dream Lands made everything much simpler, but it wasn't the only way to go about it.

Some people find their way by accident while others are well practiced in the art of lucid dreaming and are capable of finding their way on their own.

The Night Watchers had a completely different method.

In their worship of the Night Gaunts, the Watchers had

learned a few things over the centuries, and one of those was the Song of the Gaunts. Night Gaunts were mostly intelligent beings, smarter than most children and with a basic need to feed on lost souls. That same intelligence makes them impossible to control, but if one knows the Song of the Gaunts they could work out an agreement with the Gaunts.

It wouldn't be a verbal agreement. The spell is basically a telepathic call to the Gaunt. The Night Gaunt's curiosity doesn't allow it to ignore the call and within seconds you are confronted by the beast. If you're in my home reality it's just a matter of waiting for it to snatch you up and take you to the Dream Lands.

If you're in the Dream Lands, it becomes a little harder. Its faceless visage eyes you up and down and you have that moment to present a compelling telepathic argument for why it should help you.

That's where the complication comes. What can you offer a Night Gaunt? They feed on distress and emotions, so the best argument you can have to is to raise Hell wherever it is you end up. The Gaunt will then hang around and feed off that emotional discharge without ever having to inspire the terror of the kidnappings that is usually required. It's a cheap lunch.

Of course, you could always promise to give the Night Gaunt what it wants and then choose to not deliver, but then you would be constantly looking over your shoulder for a very hungry Night Gaunt.

This ancient boy wanted the Song of the Gaunts, and to use it he would most definitely cause havoc every time he came to our world. The spell would give him the power to ride in the bodies of the sleeping and comatose, anyone that a Night Gaunt would have influence over. If I didn't give him what he wanted I would be faced with a very long and drawn out search to discover information about Dyer.

Olivia could see me wrestling with the idea as the ancient boy watched us both.

"Do it! Give him the spell or our trip here was a waste of time," she hissed. There was fear in her voice and it sounded out of place. I was starting to understand that an Olivia free from the shackles of my mind was a different beast altogether.

I looked Olivia in the eyes. "Could you defeat him?"

Olivia took on a look that I wasn't familiar with seeing on her: Fear.

"No," she whispered, and shook her head quickly.

Mentally, I added this ancient boy to my already too long list of creatures to destroy, and looked back toward his little shack.

"Alright, I'll give you the damned spell." I shouted louder than I had intended, but the boy only smiled.

He walked toward us while saying. "Dr. Doran, I understand the moral quandary that this poses to you and I am more than willing to compensate you for your concern." The ancient boy stopped before us. "I have already promised to tell you where you can find your answers, but for your troubles I am also willing to provide you with the transportation required to locate the individual who will be aiding you." He smiled his creepy smile up at me. "As I am sure that you're aware, time is different here, and the sooner we can get you to your answers, the sooner you can get home to your body."

I spent what felt like the next twenty or so minutes teaching the guttural words of the song to the ancient boy as well as explaining the types of images and promises he would have to work to make the deal work. I should have just skipped the second part, because, as I expected, he already knew the deal he would have to make and only needed to know the command.

I kept my eyes mostly averted of the horrid monster. I have faced my fair share of creatures, including Night Gaunts, but they can usually sense something when they're near me, as if I am a predator, and react accordingly. We were fortunate that this one threw its eyeless gaze my direction only once that I noticed before focusing on the ancient boy entirely.

He practiced it then and I was amazed with how the beast that arrived didn't tear him apart when, instead of riding it to the world of my birth, he simply sent it away.

Oh yes, this ancient boy was going to be a very dangerous foe at some unfortunate later date.

While the beast's wings were still audible in this reality, the ancient boy returned his attention to Olivia and me.

"I am a man of my word. Please follow me." He led us back

into his shack where he turned around to face us.

The false child eyed Olivia for about the hundredth time, but this time he didn't stop himself from toying with us. "So many people in your head, Dr. Doran. Would you be willing to house another?" I felt as though he was trying to anger Olivia, but she didn't take the bait.

"More powerful beings than you have tried." I knocked on my skull. "No room for rent, sorry." I glanced around his place again and this time the place was well lit. I noticed the snowy scene outside of the windows for the first time. Everything was covered in a thick layer of mid-winter snow. I glanced back toward the still opened door and took note of the beautiful spring day and tall grasses.

This time, I managed to avoid looking like a tourist and instead jumped straight into business. "How can we find our man?"

The ancient boy looked at me with mock confusion before smacking his forehead lightly as if just remembering. "Come with me."

He walked back to the door that we had just entered and slammed it shut. Then, just as quickly, he threw it open.

I couldn't hide my surprise this time. Outside the house was a bustling city and a completely different, and much grayer, sky.

"Three blocks from here, you will find a creature that calls itself 'Timothy.' He will have all of the answers that you seek."

Olivia asked, "How are you certain that Timothy will know what we need?"

The ancient boy looked slightly annoyed as he answered. "Do you seek the whereabouts of Dr. William Dyer?"

Olivia's face contorted, first with shock and then rage. I experienced no real surprise. I had come to expect that this gentleman child knew much more than he was letting on.

"I will take your silence as confirmation." He pointed again out the door. "Timothy will have your answer. Also," he added, "I have a free piece of advice for both of you."

Concern washed over me. He didn't seem like someone who gave away anything.

"Timothy is a talker. He loves to chat with just about anyone at all, no matter their political orientation. He relished the chance to speak with several Germans this morning."

That was incredibly useful information that he had just given us. The Nazis had been here already. They had already found out where Dyer was. On the one hand, we were in second place in this race, but on the other hand, we were on the right course.

"And now," the ancient boy continued, "a piece of advice for only one of you." Before we could ask what he meant by that, Olivia was tossed out of the door by an invisible force. Before she could get to her feet, the door slammed shut.

I spun on the child and my pistol, which I hadn't brought with me, was suddenly in my hand and pointed at him.

"Put the toy away, Doctor. If I had wanted you dead, you would have been long before now." The child waved a hand dismissively at the door. "I simply wanted to share some information with you ... and only you."

I chose against lowering the gun. I had learned a long time ago that people's lips moved much more freely with a gun pointed at them than not.

He frowned at me, but continued. "Ask yourself this; with your ... friend ... outside the door, if you were to return to your body in this very moment, what would you find?"

I didn't reply, but I was fairly sure that he wasn't expecting me to. This was something for me to think on.

I had needed Olivia to get me to the Dream Lands, but if I was to find my way back without her, maybe with the help of a Night Gaunt, she would remain behind. In this new reality, Olivia and I had become separate entities. If I was to return home without her, my head would be mine again.

The downside to that idea was that I couldn't keep her in the Dream Lands, and the last thing that I wanted was for an angry and betrayed Olivia to return to taking up residence in my head.

The ancient child must have been able to read my mind, because he responded at that moment by saying, "Timothy will ask for payment. He is powerful and can hold her."

As the ancient boy said it, a wave of guilt filled me. Could I really do that to her?

The root of that question was whether or not Olivia was an individual soul, or simply an extension of myself. Would I be selling a person, or would I be simply cutting off a finger? Was she a mind, or the tumor that needed to be excised?

"Why are you telling me this?" I demanded. The ancient boy had already stated that everything had a cost. What was the cost of this piece of invaluable information?

He shrugged at me, and those small shoulders made it look more like an imitated action than any real sort of curiosity. "She is a being of power, but she is only using what she has learned from you. Your 'Olivia' is a corrupted copy of yourself. By the looks of it, one of you is difficult enough to manage, I doubt you really want two of you."

The boy paused, but his brow furrowed with legitimate concern. "While you don't need two of you, others might. An Andrew Doran with a strong will and his own mind is useless to your enemies, but an Andrew Doran with a child's potential for corruption could tip the balance of the scales." He nodded toward the door. "A world with 'her' in it, is a world that does not fit well with my concerns. Removing her from you does us both a favor."

I lowered my pistol, but kept a tight grip on it. "How do I know that you and Timothy aren't planning that same thing?"

His eerie smile returned. "You don't, but you can see how easily I can manipulate those in my home. If I wanted her, I would take her."

The finality with which that child's ancient eyes said it left me with no doubts. He could hold either of us indefinitely, but he didn't want to. It was as simple as that.

Very suddenly, I was no longer in the small shack. Instead, I was standing in the marketplace directly next to Olivia and the shack was gone. I spun around looking for it, but it was nowhere to be seen.

Olivia grabbed me by the shoulders, and a wild anger had filled her eyes. "What was that about? What did he tell you?"

With more force than was necessary, I shoved her away from me. I jabbed my index finger in her direction. "You don't get to make demands of me. I'll tell you what I want when I'm good and ready." I didn't like how little control I was in while in the Dream Lands, and Olivia's inability to be inside my head was obviously wearing on her. She didn't like being kept out of the loop that had made up the entirety of her existence.

Realizing that she lost control of herself in her panic, Olivia nodded, but I could tell that she didn't like it one bit.

That's when I made my decision. I just didn't care what she thought. The ancient boy had said that she was a corrupted copy of myself. That made sense with everything I had managed to piece together since learning the truth about her.

Olivia was a corrupted piece of me that craved power, which explained why she was always encouraging me to use it. It was why she had helped me to cross Europe. It had all been an effort to get me to use more and more of my power. All while driving me crazier and making herself stronger. She only cared for me in that I could make her stronger.

As these thoughts crossed my mind, it also occurred to me how nice it would be to have my life and magic back under my own control. That thought sealed my decision for me. Timothy would help me, and if not, I would shackle her to a damned wall before I left.

We followed the ancient child's directions, walking the marketplace. All around us were magics and creatures that even I had never seen or heard of before. Large bipedal plants were selling memories in translucent jars at one stand, while at another a faceless dog was offering to augment your body in the Dream Lands. The people that spoke to the dog would step up, trade some sort of black crystal, devoid of any reflection, and be instantly transformed. One such being, a man as far as I could tell, traded the crystal and was immediately changed. Gills sprouted from his neck, his eyes bulged to a wider and more fish-like shape, and his arms were replaced with tentacles all within the blink of an eye.

As we made our way through the narrow streets, Olivia and I noticed that up ahead the crowd had begun giving a wide berth to something. When we stepped closer, we saw that it was a Child of Dreams.

The results of being born in the Dream Lands to parents

from a different reality was that the Dream Lands had only a very basic template to work with, and the children always came out … unnatural.

This woman was no different. She walked, naked, through the marketplace. While her body was that of an ordinary woman, it was the only thing ordinary about her. Her age changed with each step she took. In one moment she was in her mid-thirties and in the next she was well over the age of eighty. Her next steps saw her change from old to a young girl to old again and then to a baby. She cried once before returning to the woman in her thirties.

What also made her uncomfortable to be around was that from every angle she also looked a different height and weight. The world that she'd been born into hadn't been prepared for creating a being from scratch and had opted to create a being that was some sort of odd amalgamation of all versions of that being. It was saddening, but not nearly as sad as the look in her eyes.

All of her other features, in every state of change, were completely human, but her eyes lacked something and it was clear to see that the something missing was why people gave her such a wide area. She had no morality and no understanding. She was taking in the entire world around her, yet none of it was retained. Her devoid gaze was so alien that you could see the powers behind it. This Child of Dreams contained the ability to unmake the world around her if she so chose, but instead walked through it.

It was why so many people were keeping their distance. No one wanted to be the person or creature that aroused the ire of someone who could unmake them.

I had been so enthralled this creature that I hadn't realized that Olivia had stepped away from me or that I had almost walked right up to her. It crossed my mind then that I was once again in the mode of tourist and it was about to get me killed.

As soon as I realized the predicament I had put myself in, I made motion to remove myself from it, but it was too late.

"Doctor Andrew Doran," she said to me and it was in a thousand voices, all shifting through different pitches. "It is a pleasure to see you again."

"I'm sorry," I said, carefully, "but, have we met?"

This woman with brown, red, blonde, and gray hair giggled, and it was a terrifying sound unlike anything that I had ever heard before. Like a train crashing into a thousand cats.

She reached for my hand, and it took everything in my power not to flinch. "No, Doctor, it is I who am sorry. My people, as you've helped me to learn, exist outside of conventional time. This would be your first meeting with me, but not mine."

As she held my hand, I noticed that she stopped phasing in and out of bodies and her voice became only one. Before me stood a tall and graceful woman with blonde hair who looked to be in her early forties.

The comfortability that she had with me helped me to calm down. This was a woman who trusted me, therefore, I felt as though I could trust her.

"What is your name?" I asked her.

She giggled again, and this time it was a simple giggle with an innocent child-like quality to it.

"My name is impossible for you to pronounce, but you have taken to calling me Annie."

I smiled. "Well, it is a pleasure to meet you, Annie."

She nodded. "I will be afraid when it is my turn to meet you. Be yourself, and don't give up on me."

I returned the nod and watched as her gaze slid over my shoulder.

The smile stayed on her lips but fled from her eyes. "Andrew, is that her? The being of your mind?"

I knew what she meant. She had seen Olivia. "Yes," was all I could think to say.

"Then today is the day of your decision." Annie brought her eyes back to mine, and the previously soulless gaze I thought that I had seen was completely gone. This was a being who had known love and concern.

"Stay strong, Doctor. In the coming weeks your decision will haunt you, but I truly believe that you made … will make … the correct one."

"Haunt me?" I asked, suddenly concerned.

Annie's smile widened. "You told me not to share such things with you, and now I see why. You linear-folk are incapable of handling well-meant advice." She pulled me into a hug and I tried to ignore the nakedness pressed against me. "I will leave you now to forge that path that will bring you into my life. The most powerful thing Andrew Doran ever did was remain true to himself."

In that instant I was standing alone in the marketplace filled with confusion and annoyance. Confusion at the portents of my future, and annoyance that everyone here could vanish at will except for me.

Olivia was by my side again, and I was very aware of her wanting to ask me what the entire scene had been about, so I threw her a bone. "I guess she's from my future." Olivia's gaze changed to one of concern and I smiled. "She's a friend. Her name is Annie."

The people all around were keeping their distance from us now. Fear filled their eyes and I could see that, while I couldn't disappear at will, being friends with a Child of Dreams was a thing of power. These people feared me. That would work to my advantage, I hoped.

We walked another block before Olivia's very obvious frustration began to annoy me. "What is going on?" I demanded.

She replied by returning the shove I had given her earlier. "You're not telling me everything!" Olivia screamed. "I ... I am..." she frowned as she searched for the word, "disconnected. I can't just pull clues from your consciousness. I am not used to you keeping secrets from me!" She began crying as rage flooded her eyes and stamping her feet. "What did that boy in the shack tell you?" she demanded again.

I stepped right up to her and laughed in her face.

"You immature child!" I prodded. "You aren't a person without me. How much of me do you use to make you? My maturity? My memories? You're so used to having so much access to my mind that when you finally have a life of your own you throw a tantrum." I stepped back as she cried harder. "What is it? You don't like being out and about? Building memories and thoughts for yourself for once?"

Olivia looked around the marketplace and wiped her tears.

"It is nice to be out, but I am so much less than I was."

"Wrong!" I shouted. "You're so much more! You're independent and free to live your own choices instead of mine. You're not a voice in the back of a head, you're free! You're ... oh!" It suddenly hit me. "You're lonely? One voice in your head isn't enough for you?"

She began glowering at me then and sticking out her bottom lip, but I continued. "Well, no worries, because the sooner we find this Timothy character and find out what he knows about our man Dyer, the sooner we can get back to our regular routine."

Olivia seemed to calm down immensely at that, but added. "You could still tell me what he said to you. Or what that dream girl said."

Ignorant, childish, and immature when she was outside of my head, I figured that meant gullible as well. "He wanted to buy you off me. I told him that nobody gets a piece of me and then I demanded to be released." I poured conviction into my voice and watched as Olivia's eyes went from cautious distrust to trust. She had taken the bait.

"My hero." Olivia was smiling and wiping away the last of her tears.

I rolled my eyes and added. "He already had my Night Gaunt spell, he didn't need access to anything else that I might know."

Olivia feigned pain at the implied insult, but I could tell that she was pleased with me and my lie.

We walked another block in silence, her frustration having abated, before we finally reached where I could only suppose Timothy resided.

There was a ragged cough to our right and we turned to check it out since nothing else of interest existed in this area. There was a large stack of rags and torn cloth that stood at least as tall as myself and twice as wide.

Without any sort of fear, but a little bit of excitement, I stepped up to it and asked, "Timothy?"

A loud noise that could only be described as a belch erupted from the rags and they tremored gently.

A high-pitched voice said, "Dr. Doran, I have waited so long for the winds to carry you to my shores."

I skipped the pleasantries and stated very plainly. "Is there anyone in this damned world who doesn't know who I am?"

"That is not the question that you have come to ask me." Timothy replied.

"No," I frowned. "Where can we find William Dyer?"

The rags shook again. "I can tell you where your colleague is. It will, of course, cost you."

"I understand."

"Do you?" Timothy asked in his high voice. "Were you told the price?"

I nodded and ignored the confused look that crossed Olivia's face.

"Your Dr. Dyer sings the song of the lonely in the Blasted Heath. He shakes in fear at the legend of colour and locks himself away."

"What does that even mean?" Olivia demanded, but I cut her off by raising my hand.

"I know where he is." I told her.

"What?" Olivia demanded. "Where is he?"

Timothy was suddenly shaking much more violently than he had previously. "May I have my payment now?"

Nervous that I might get double-crossed, I nodded and said, "You may collect at any time."

The confusion on Olivia's face was quickly turning to frustration after I said that. She spun to me to ask again what the payment was, but she wasn't fast enough.

A section of the rag pile shifted and a scarred eyestalk popped out of the top of the cloth. At that same time, two black and purple tentacles as thick as my leg and covered with brown suckers shot forth from the base of the stack of rags and grabbed Olivia's legs.

Even with her supernatural strength, she was no match for them as they dragged her back toward Timothy.

Olivia's initial reaction was complete terror until her eyes fell on me. When she saw my complete lack of surprise, or maybe my complete lack of action to defend her, her eyes were filled with a sad look of betrayal.

Before she was pulled into the rags, I saw a quick flash of rage fill her eyes.

Then Olivia was gone.

"You should go now," Timothy said under strain. His still visible eyestalk was bulging with the effort of subduing Olivia.

"Can you hold her?" I asked.

"Easily, but you should leave." Was all that Timothy said before retracting his eyestalk back within the rags.

There was a sharp sound behind me, and I spun to see what it was. There was nothing there, but when I spun back, Olivia and Timothy had completely vanished and I was alone on that block of the marketplace.

It didn't take me long to decide that I didn't want to be in the Dream Lands any longer.

Quickly and quietly, I mumbled the Song of the Gaunts and waited for the strong, hooked feet of the Night Gaunt to grab me by the shoulders.

Focusing my will, I guided the beast back to my body.

Chapter 4: The Blasted Heath

I awoke with little memory of the return trip to my body. The only thing that I remembered was the sudden drop before my eyes fluttered open.

Unlike normal sleep, I wasn't feeling any more rested than I had been before I took my trek into the Dream Lands. I had been concerned that the beastly Night Gaunt would have fought my commands and stolen me away into wherever it is that Night Gaunts nest. The chance of me never returning to the waking world was greater than I cared to admit, even to myself.

The elation I felt from being back in my body and in my office lasted only until I opened my eyes. It took me a moment to realize what I was looking at. My eyes took in the obvious forms of Leo and the new girl, Nancy Dyer, but then I realized that they were kneeling in front of my desk with their hands behind their heads. Directly behind them were two larger men, with equally large pistols, in the basic clothing you would see on anyone in the school. They were hiding among the students. There was one more man guarding the door. He carried no gun.

I instantly moved to jump up from my seat when a strong hand clasped my shoulder and forced me back down.

"Relax, Doctor. You're not going anywhere."

I glanced to my right at the man who had spoken and still held my shoulder. He was dressed as the others, but wore a button vest. He held his pistol in the other hand, not aimed at anywhere in particular.

I spun my head to my left and realized that Mr. Vest didn't need to aim his pistol anywhere, because the largest of the four men, stretching the limits of his Miskatonic University sweater, held another pistol, incredibly small in his immense hands, near my temple.

To say the least, I was intimidated…

…but I sure as Hell wasn't going to let them see that.

"Get that damned gun out of my face!" I shouted at Mr. Mountain on my left. He didn't move, and that left me with only Plan B.

I sighed heavily. "More Yig worshipers. Really? I would have thought that the Nazis had a higher standard of cultists lying about." I nodded toward Leo. "I miss the days of Cthulhu Cultists. Boy! Did they know how to throw a punch. Am I right, Leo?"

At first his eyes looked totally bewildered as my message was temporarily lost in translation, but he quickly caught on and laughed. "And they carried bigger guns," he added.

I noticed out of the corner of my eye as Mr. Vest looked from me to Leo and then back to me. I could tell he was surprised that I saw through his disguise, but I wanted to make him stew as his curiosity fought with his dignity. The longer he waited, the better.

When I finally felt that enough time had passed to where it was almost becoming awkward instead of intimidating to be sitting in that silence, I nodded toward Mr. Mountain's gun hand.

"Your scales are showing." The cuff of his sweater came almost up to his palm, but it didn't cover enough. The guard's wrist had light green scales blending into the skin of his palm. I had noticed it when I first took in Mr. Mountain's insanely large form.

Mr. Mountain looked down to where I had nodded and I didn't wait. I slapped the gun up, hitting the base of his scaled hand and ducking down. The gun fired, as I expected it to, and I kicked back with my chair. The chair in the Dean's office was on casters, and I rolled back and bounced into the wall. As I did, I lifted my head and saw that the bullet from Mr. Mountain's misfire had cut into the shoulder of Mr. Vest.

Mr. Vest had plenty to deal with in regard to his leaking arm, so I leapt to my feet and punched the still surprised Mr.

Mountain in the jaw. I thought my hand broke as I did it and Mr. Mountain looked more annoyed than actually hurt, so I punched him again. That time his eyes filled with rage and he swung his gun arm toward me.

I grabbed a letter opener from the desk and jabbed out and toward his scale-covered wrist. The blade sliced into the scaled skin and he dropped the gun. I scooped it up before it hit the floor. Standing, I took aim at Mr. Vest.

The other three guards hadn't moved during any of my altercation, and they hadn't needed to. My plan hadn't been escape, only to sting. With one follower of Yig on the door and one with a pistol to the head of each of my companions, I had very few options aside from surrender.

I still needed just a little more time.

"Drop the gun and sit down," barked the Yig worshiper guarding Nancy. "Or we will kill your people."

I didn't move. He knew we were at a stalemate, so I called him out on it. "You won't do that, and we all know it." I watched as the guard glanced down at his charge and knew I was right. "You already know who she is, and you are going to need her if you can't find Dyer."

Nancy's guard aimed his pistol at Leo's head. "We do not need the Frenchman."

I nodded but I didn't lower my gun. "If he dies, I'll kill you all before another bullet can leave the gun." The coldness in my voice had the desired effect and they didn't shoot Leo, but they also didn't move.

Nancy's guard, Mr. Chatter, with his gun still aimed at Leo, decided to keep talking. "At best you could get one of us before we gunned you down."

Laughing, I lifted my gun away from them slowly before dropping it.

The gun started to drop before stopping and floating into place pressed lightly against Mr. Mountain's forehead. "Do you have any idea where you are?"

Mr. Chatter took on a look of confusion, and for the first time since he had started talking, Mr. Chatter was speechless.

I crossed my arms over my chest. Holding the gun in

place with my magic was more of a parlor trick than anything. Moving objects was one of the easier spells, but holding them in place for any length of time could be tiring. I hid it from my face as I spoke.

"This isn't the Dean's office in some random private university. This is *Miskatonic University*. It's the largest collection of volatile and arcane magics from all over the world!" I barked another laugh. "You are standing in a city that has been referred to as a hub for every vile creature that has roamed this planet!"

Mr. Chatter asked, "What does any of that even mean?" He shot a confused glance at his nearest companion.

"It means," I smiled, "that my local *Wendigo* is the most dedicated secretary in the business!"

Something vaguely human-shaped fell from the ceiling and onto Mr. Chatter. A fount of blood shot from the fast moving mass of Wendigo and Mr. Chatter. His companions only stared, terrified by the sight before them.

The Wendigo has been a creature mostly spoken about by the American Indians. They were part of folklore among many different groups for generations. The Indians knew that excessive cannibalism would transform a person. They would become stronger and take on the ability to shape shift. The Wendigo form varied based on the environment, but generally they became gray-skinned with bright red eyes and sharp claws and teeth. The strength of the Wendigo, absorbed and multiplied by the people it consumed, was only matched by its speed. They were fast, strong, and able to hide in plain sight as normal people. They were the perfect hunters of man.

Standing from the mess of gore on the floor, a gray-skinned and very sharp-toothed and clawed Carol Berg stretched her neck. Her eyes were filled with the red of her natural form.

"Thank you for noticing my dedication, sir." She frowned at me, and I found myself wanting to shrink away. "I will, of course, still need you to sign the renovation agreements for Pellman Hall." I nodded, because it was either that or shake in terror. Thank goodness she was on our side.

Carol's hand flashed out and returned in another spray of blood as she took out the throat of the guard standing behind

Leo. "For now, Doctor, I suggest that we table the renovation agreements." She lifted her head and sniffed the air. "More are coming. Weapon-up, soldier, you must leave."

In a puddle of his own bodily fluids, the guard at the door finally snapped out of his terror long enough to look out the door. Before I could see the look of relief on his face at the sight of the Yig cavalry, Carol Berg had already removed his head.

Mr. Vest had begun pleading with me to shoot him before my blood-soaked secretary made it to him. I grabbed the floating gun from the air and slammed the butt of it into his nose and watched him crumple on the floor.

His companion, Mr. Mountain, took the moment to yank the letter opener from his wrist and leap at me. Unfortunately for him, mountains lack speed, and I put him down with a bullet.

I grabbed Mr. Vest's gun from the floor and tossed both pistols to Leo, who proceeded to check them before passing one to Nancy. I heard him mumble, "You are with us now," as I stepped toward the bookshelf.

Rearing back, I kicked the bottom shelf of the ceiling high bookshelf. The shelf of fake tomes at chest level slid in and then up, revealing a secret compartment where I kept my cavalry sword and .38 revolver.

I quickly strapped on my holster and scabbard, sliding the weapons into their sheaths.

Turning back to my companions, I noticed Nancy staring at my rune-covered pistol.

"What is it?" I asked, suddenly wondering what about my gun had put that wide-eyed look on her face.

"Is that..." she hesitated with doubt. "Is that the *Equalizer*?"

I raised an eyebrow as Leo asked, "The what?"

Noise in the hall stopped Nancy from answering as I ushered us all toward the window. I glanced at Leo, "Where's the book?"

Leo turned his gaze back to Nancy who pulled the small journal from a back pocket. Leo yanked it from her grip faster than she could pull it away and tossed it to me.

"Thank you," I said.

Nancy began waving her newly acquired pistol around

while she spoke. "You'll trust me with a gun but not the book?"

I looked at her while Leo climbed out of the window. "Do you have no idea where you are?" I waved my own hands around then. "Do I have to give that whole speech again? This entire University was built on the foundation that books are more dangerous than guns. This whole situation is over *that* book. So, yes! I trust you with a gun more than I trust you with a book that contains the half-mad firsthand account of an alien culture that the entire Third Reich is after!" I sighed as Yig worshipers began coming into the room and meeting Carol. "At least with the gun all that you can do is kill me." I waved at the window. "Sometime today, please."

Nancy frowned at me and another Yig screamed. The mixture of snake-like hiss and terrified death-screams made him sound like a tea kettle at boil.

Nancy peeked out the window to gauge the distance. It was only about a ten foot drop. She slid over the sill and dropped.

I tossed a quick glance over my shoulder to see how Carol was faring and regretted it immediately. That gory vision would haunt my nightmares for a very long time. I left her to her carnage playground and jumped out of the window to land beside Leo and Nancy as they brushed themselves off.

Leo's truck keys are in his hand from seemingly nowhere. "Where are we headed?"

I nodded toward his hand before looking at the window we just fell from. "Your truck, obviously, and quickly, I would assume."

We took off at a jog, with Leo in the lead.

"Where will we take the truck?" Leo asked with a hint of his usual annoyance in his voice.

"I think that I know where Dr. Dyer is, I'll direct you."

Nancy grabbed my arm then and yanked me around. Leo halted to see why we had stopped moving. "Where's my father?"

I frowned at her. "I told you, I'll direct Leo to take us there."

"How did you find him?" Leo interrupted Nancy's death stare.

"I haven't yet, and I hadn't planned on the Germans using more of those damnable Yig. Now if we could please continue to the truck…" I moved to run, but was stopped again by Nancy's hand on my arm.

"I asked you where my father was. Tell me." I noticed her grip tightening on the pistol and wondered exactly how half-cocked this girl really was.

I hesitated just a little too long and Nancy slapped me across the face.

I rubbed my cheek. "Your father's in the Blasted Heath!" I hissed through gritted teeth. I half hoped that the Yig would have heard, not to give them a sporting chance with Dyer's location, but to have them rate my hissed reply on a scale of one to "Yig."

A sudden crash and a howl of pain, sounding unfortunately similar to what I assumed Carol Berg might make, echoed down from the window and across to us.

Nancy began to ask me what the Blasted Heath was, but it was my turn to be demanding. "Not now. Get. To. The. Truck." I said before turning our previous jog into a sprint that followed closely on the heels of the Frenchman.

In just a few minutes, we crossed the campus and were in the cab of Leo's clunker of a truck.

I didn't tell Leo how to get to the Blasted Heath. We needed to make certain that we weren't leading the Nazis snake-lackeys directly to William Dyer's location. I left Leo to weave between the different roads throughout Arkham. I only directed him to head generally northwest. Anything more specific could wait. I explained that to Nancy in the hopes of calming her down.

As far as she knew, we were really close to finally reuniting her with her father. I didn't have the heart to tell her that the reunion might not be what she hoped it to be.

I was also concerned about exactly how much Timothy had told the Germans. Those Yig worshipers had been in my school for weeks. I recognized two of them from the halls. They had obviously been tasked with keeping an eye on me, but what triggered them to act when they did? Was it the presence of Nancy Dyer on school grounds, or was it the fact that Timothy had finally given them the information that they required?

The answer meant a world of difference. If it was Nancy's

sudden appearance, then they must have known who she was. I was willing to blame Brandon Smythe for that slip up.

If, instead, the Nazis had learned as much as I had from Timothy, then the Yig worshipers that we had been waylaid by would be only a part of a larger force. The rest would be awaiting our arrival in the Blasted Heath.

As if that wasn't enough, the Blasted Heath was something to fear as well.

Glancing over my shoulder for what felt like the thousandth time, I directed Leo to take the next left, explaining that we needed to head out of town to the northwest.

Then I steeled myself, and turned as best I could in the tight cab to face Nancy who sat tightly between Leo and myself.

"Nancy, the Blasted Heath isn't just a place to hide," I began.

She looked up at me with a sharp look that implied that she didn't need protecting. This wasn't going to be easy to explain, so I jumped right in.

Or tried to, anyway. As I opened my mouth, Leo interrupted.

"How did you discover that Dr. Dyer was in this 'Blasted Heath'?"

I took a deep breath and recounted my journey through the Dream Lands, being extra careful not to mention Olivia. From the look on Leo's face as he drove, I figured he understood that Olivia had been with me. Nancy, for her credit, didn't question my walking through a parallel reality. At least, she didn't question it out loud.

I ended the recounting with Timothy, the many-tentacled thing wrapped in rags, and added, for Leo's sake, "That was when I was able to leave behind all of my problems and found out where Nancy's father was hiding." I put emphasis on 'leave behind,' and watched as Leo's eyes registered a moment of surprise, then confusion, and finally confused acceptance.

He didn't press the issue, and I was certain that a bottle of bourbon and a moment to breathe would get me telling him exactly how I had betrayed my insanity and left her to rot in the Dream Lands.

"With your father hiding in the Blasted Heath," I said to Nancy, "he might not be of any use to us or the Nazis."

A moment of fear crossed her eyes as she asked, "What does that mean?"

"The Blasted Heath isn't a great place to hide because of the deep woods and hills. It's a great place to hide because something lives there. Something … alien. It lives deep in the ground and its presence has been wreaking havoc on the fabric between our reality and what I like to refer to as the void."

"The void?" She asked.

I thought I saw Leo roll his eyes as I took a deep breath and began to explain.

"The void is what I call the reality that shares the same space as ours, only on a different plane of existence. The void is accessible to those with special gifts, or those who have seen the path to the void before. It's right here, next to us, and only kept separate by a thin barrier between the two realities that I call the veil, for simplification.

"The monsters that your father saw, and the monsters that people dream of or that roam our world are all creatures from beyond that veil. When the veil lifts, these beasts can escape and they don't always follow the rules of our reality. The creature that exists in the Blasted Heath, for example. From what I've gleaned from the stories, the creature is a being of energy, and appears as an indescribable color. Its decades-long presence in the Blasted Heath hasn't lifted the veil, but has thinned it. Things leak through the Blasted Heath and claw at people's minds."

Nancy looked more confused than shocked. "So, there are monsters in the Blasted Heath? What does that have to do with my father?"

I shook my head. "No, the monsters are still in the veil, but they can cast their minds out into the Heath, and the only thing those minds can touch are other minds. Like ours. Like your fathers."

Leo grunted and I knew that he had caught on to what I was trying to say.

"For the most part, the place is completely safe. All of these monster minds reaching out of the Blasted Heath create an aura that humans can sense. We avoid the place at all costs and most people don't even know why." I sighed. "But the Blasted Heath's aura can't stop people who are specifically trying to get inside it. Your father knew what it was, or he would never have tried to hide there. The aura would protect him from prying eyes, and how thin the veil is would protect him from any sort of magical detection. In that regard he was completely safe."

"'That regard'?" Nancy pressed.

I nodded. "For all your father has seen, he's still human and he's been missing for months. Even I couldn't last months in there without completely losing my battle to the void. Your father won't be the man you knew when you last saw him. He'll have had his mind warped either to their influence, or his constant struggle to keep them out will have put him into a catatonic state, where he keeps everything, from both realities, out. William Dyer won't be of much use to anyone in there."

Nancy started hitting me in the chest with her elbow as much as the awkward closeness would allow. "You don't even know what you're talking about. He wouldn't hide somewhere that would destroy him!"

I put my arm up to block her hits. "I hope that you're right, but it isn't likely. Our best hope is that he still retains enough of himself that in time he could return to being a functional person."

"*Merde.*" Leo cursed.

"Damn you!" Nancy threw a glance at Leo and shouted, "Damn both of you." She returned her eyes to me. "You don't know my father. You don't know the type of man he is. He survived that horrible place that you read about because he is a survivor. He will always survive because that is the type of man that he is!"

I had obviously challenged the image that Nancy had of her father and I felt immediately guilty for it. I was trying to prepare her for the truth, when I probably should have been comforting her. Nancy had already come to expect the worst, and her entire journey to find her father was an act of fanning the flames of her own hope.

"You're right." Leo, always the gentleman, was attempting to save face before I even could. "We do not know your father, but we are trying to help."

Nancy remained quiet, so I took up the torch. "Either way, we need to be prepared for when we enter. Your father might have survived the creatures that dwell in the void, but I am not so certain that we will."

"What do you mean?" Leo asked, obvious relief at the change of subject flashing across his face.

"Those creatures that slither into our brains from the void will be trying to gain purchase and anchor themselves to us. We won't be there long enough for it to be permanent, but they will manipulate our minds and our emotions all in an effort to make us their avatars in this world. We won't be them, but we could become puppeted by them."

Panic crossed both of my companion's faces, and I tried to explain. "For the most part, aside from some strain, I will be fine. I have enough practice with the void that this will be a very simple sparring match. To that regard, Leo will have little to contend with as well, but, unfortunately, his resistance will be nothing like mine. Leo will most likely be distracted and quick to temper." Leo frowned but kept his eyes on the road. "Nancy, you are the one I am the most concerned about."

Her panic intensified and I made a quick note that Leo should be the one to explain things to her from that point forward.

"You have no practice with the void, and this will make you susceptible to its influence," I explained.

Her face paling, Nancy asked, "What will it do to me?"

I shrugged, suddenly wishing I hadn't. "They can manipulate emotions and thoughts if you can't resist them, and guessing their agenda is impossible. We simply won't know until you are in the Heath."

Looking at Nancy, I knew I wasn't helping, so I tried a different tact.

"If you force yourself to focus on your goal, it will be harder for the void to find purchase in your mind. Focus on finding your father. It won't stop them and they will try to control you, but as long as you focus on finding your father, they can't own you."

I poured confidence in my voice, but I doubted that she bought it.

"How will we find Dyer?" Leo asked.

This time, I was the one grateful for the subject change. "We will ask a local," I answered.

"You just said that no one lives in the Blasted Heath," Nancy countered.

"Almost no one." I sighed. "There are always exceptions to the rules. The Blasted Heath ... the things reaching through the void managed to get their hold on one man. He held onto his own will for much longer than I suspect even I could. In the end he succumbed. They wiggled into his mind and turned him into their puppet. He speaks for them and I don't think there's much of the original man left aside from the shell that is his flesh."

"Who is this man?" Leo asked.

"Ammi Pierce," I supplied. "When the thing under the ground first came, Ammi was one of the first to have direct contact with it. He knew the people whose well that it had fallen into, but when they disappeared, and the rest of the people of the Heath had left, he stayed. I don't know how long he's been there, but I'll bet that the void will keep his body from failing him."

"He can't die?" Nancy was obviously trying to forget about the earlier horrors that I had suggested, so I indulged her.

"I'm sure that his body could be destroyed, but death as we know it wouldn't make any difference. The void would just choose another to house their collective will." I lowered my voice, only a little. "Try not to forget: Ammi speaks for the creatures reaching through the void, but the creature beneath the Blasted Heath has no voice. There will be two beings, at least, hiding your father."

There was really nothing that Nancy could say after everything that I had told her, and while she was scared, she seemed to be accepting it all. That was odd, but relieving. If I was right about her father, we were going to need her even more.

We rode in silence for a few more miles before I saw the haze ahead of us. It was the presence of the void I had previously mentioned. Those who couldn't sense the void's presence wouldn't see anything, but I saw a fog with an unknown color to it. It reminded me of a purple bruise.

Leo put on the brakes as we approached it, slowing as it came into his less focused senses. He glanced at me and I provided him a nod, encouraging him to drive through it. He mumbled "*Merde*," again and took his foot off the brakes.

Nancy didn't seem to notice, and I watched her as we crossed into the presence of the void.

In my own mind, I felt the things reaching into and through me. Indescribable creatures existed in the periphery of my vision and their inky tendrils slid across the surface of my mind. They grasped at any stray thoughts they could find, so I gave them the same defense I always did: Baseball.

My defenses against the void were to give them things they couldn't use, and as a child I had thoroughly enjoyed playing baseball. As the void reached for me, I played an imaginary game in my mind. I hit the ball and rounded the bases. Of course, over the years I had built up my other mental defenses, turning my mind into a walled fortress, but even a fortress needed a moat, and that was baseball.

Nancy didn't have baseball, and while I was hitting home runs, I watched as Nancy's eyelids lowered halfway and her body untensed completely. She sagged between Leo and me as the creatures of the void played with her pliable mind.

Leo had a very different reaction. As we drove into the mist, his face tensed and his brow furrowed. He had the look he took on in battle. It was concentration and focus. All Leo had was a moat, and it was going to take everything in his mind to defend against the void. He wouldn't last, but he would last longer than Nancy did.

"Is that a cat on the window?" Nancy suddenly asked. She pointed at the window and I frowned. This was a weird reaction. The void-beasts were testing her perceptions.

Leo looked at Nancy and then to me. His look of concentration had turned to one of general discomfort. I optimistically took that to mean that he'd managed to reach a standstill with the beasts.

The road curved as we came over another hill and the countryside began looking withered and gray. The trees had completely lost their leaves and swayed even though there had been no breeze that afternoon. There was no living vegetation on the ground, only dirt and dead grass.

A gravel road broke off to the left and I directed Leo down it. It ended in a small one-room house, eerily similar to the ancient child's shack from the Dream Lands. Behind it was a small barn. Both of the structures were in a poor state and had fallen into disrepair over the many years that Ammi Pierce had lived there.

Or, if the stories were true, they had fallen into disrepair even before that.

Leo pulled the truck to a stop directly in front of the house. Ammi Pierce stood on the remains of what used to be a front porch, watching us and not moving.

Ammi Pierce was wearing stained overalls with a surprisingly white undershirt. From his chin to just past his waistline was a long, white beard that needed to be washed. His thinning hair was just as white as his undershirt and his feet were bare. I could see his incredibly long toenails from the truck.

I started to get out of the truck when I realized that Nancy wasn't even thinking about it. Her eyes were still glazed over, but they had focused on the shell of a man standing outside. I had to remind her of her focus.

"Nancy, your father is somewhere near here. We're close, keep your eye on the ball and we will get out of here soon."

I mouthed at Leo, "Keep your eye on her." He hesitated for only a moment, obviously trying to think past the foreign thoughts clawing at his mind, before nodding in the affirmative.

To Nancy's credit, her eyes came back into focus and she forced herself to sit up straighter. "Let's get this over with," she said to no one in particular.

We all slid from the cab of the truck, and I lead the pack closer to Ammi Pierce. The only movement that he made the entire time was with his eyes as they followed us.

I started as Ammi's raspy voice barked. "You can't have him!"

Nancy and Leo started as well, and I noticed that Leo had

pulled his pistol, holding it at his side.

"You can't have him!" Ammi barked again. He added in a much quieter voice, "He's been too much fun…"

There was something just behind his vocal cords as he spoke, and I could almost hear the beasts riding his body.

"Whatever happened to you Ammi?" I asked, slowly resting my hand on my own holstered gun. "That creature didn't even land in your well."

There was a sudden confusion in Ammi's eyes and the voice that came out didn't carry with it the sounds of the creatures. "N-no. It was in … in…" he frowned as the last piece of whatever was Ammi in there tried to recall his neighbor's name. "… Nahum's. It … destroyed them."

The voices returned. "They couldn't handle the color from the stars. I couldn't either, so when the new voices began to get loud enough to understand, they made me a promise."

"They would help you keep people away from the blight, in exchange for," I waved my hand at the old man, "this?"

He nodded at us and smiled, showing his toothless mouth. "I don't need to eat or drink, and the damned blight would ruin it all for me anyway. I am eternal…" his own voice returned for only a moment, "… to … s-save Arkham."

Ammi Pierce's sacrifice made me feel sick to my stomach. This was but one beachhead in a war that raged far larger than our own world, yet Ammi stood as a dam to its torrent. They had convinced him that if he didn't stand there, taking all that they gave him, the blight would continue to spread.

It wasn't true. Unfortunately, they had lied to him. Whatever had been left behind to live in the lands of the Blasted Heath only had so much reach, and its own aura was keeping people away well enough. As it wore at the veil between realities, the voices had found the panicked and shattered soul, ripe for the picking.

It was too late to tell Ammi that. It might even damage him to do so. I had thought all that remained of the old man had been lost to the creatures, but his sense of hope had allowed him to hold onto the last pieces of his soul.

Hand still on my pistol, I didn't really care about Ammi's

story, and returned the conversation to what we really needed to know.

"Where is he?" I demanded.

Ammi's brief surfacing vanished and I was talking to the beasts in the void again. They smiled.

"There are very few places in your world that such a man could hide, but I already told you. You can't have him."

"We do not have time for this," Leo was suddenly shouting. He stepped forward quickly, lifting his pistol and taking aim at Ammi. As he stepped forward, he knocked over the clearly influenced Nancy, sending her to the ground.

Spitting as he shouted, Leo demanded in French, "Where is Dyer?"

Ammi only smiled at Leo, not afraid of what a gun might do to his body.

Annoyance filled my mind, and while some of it was mine, I recognized the influence of the void. They wanted me to drive this outburst to its seemingly inevitable conclusion. I fought through it and focused to think.

This wasn't Leo's fault any more than my annoyance was mine. I had to speak to Leo and get past the creatures' puppetry.

I stepped over Nancy who was now writhing on the ground trying to get back to her feet with no success.

"Leo, please listen to me." I was gritting my teeth as I spoke. "This isn't a man. The void needed a toy, someone to play with and entertain them. It chose Ammi. It wormed into his mind and, piece by piece, replaced and changed the man into a puppet." I sighed as some of the void's fog lifted from my mind. "He has power, more than I do when I touch the void. Why do you think he hasn't made you put the gun down yet?"

Leo frowned as confusion covered his eyes.

"Think, Leo!" I shouted. "Why hasn't he stopped you from shooting him?"

Leo's face showed his struggles to push through the void's fog on his own mind and think about the situation.

"He is not stopping me from shooting him, because he doesn't think that I will shoot him. That…" he frowned as a new idea came to him, "…or he wants me to shoot him."

I nodded. "If you shoot him, the void will choose a new toy. Of the three of us, who do you think the void will pick?" I could see that Leo wasn't getting my point, so I explained it for him. "Nancy's too easy. They would be done with her in a day." I pointed at myself. "I can resist them and if push came to shove, I might even be able to hurt them. There's only one person here would could put up enough of a fight to be entertaining." I sighed and pointed at Leo. "There's only one viable replacement for Ammi Pierce."

Leo held the gun aimed at the still smiling Ammi's face for a second longer as my words sunk in. When they did, he lowered the gun quickly and stepped away from Ammi.

Leo didn't want to be a puppet.

As he got further away from Ammi, he grabbed Nancy by the arm and pulled her to her feet. Then he looked her in the eyes and began demanding for her to focus.

That was why I liked Leo. He was a soldier in every sense of the word. He wasn't going to focus on how close to losing his mind and soul he had just come. Instead he was going to focus on making sure that no one else did. It made him a very useful ally for staying on point.

I turned away from my friend and back to the still-smiling avatar of another reality. "I, on the other hand, can do whatever the hell I want to you."

With how thin the veil between worlds was there, I was surrounded by the power of the void. Normally, my access to that power can be limited by how much work I have to put forth to grab it, but in the Blasted Heath, the void was tissue paper that I could easily tear.

I drew my sword and used the void's power to lift Ammi Pierce off the ground. I held him about a foot from the ground, incapable of retreating from what I was about to do.

The symbols carved into the black blade of the sword began to glow. I had never seen it happen before and could only assume that it was also feeling how close the other reality was.

The smile vanished from Ammi Pierce's face and he began to flail about in the air.

I pressed the tip of my magical sword against his abdomen

and watched as it sizzled and smoked the flesh underneath the cloth. I pressed harder and Ammi let out a howl.

"I believe that you can't die. Heck, I could kill the bastards riding you right now and a handful more would fill the space I emptied." I pressed the sword an inch deeper, slicing and burning flesh as I did so. "Why would I want to kill you when I could make your life hell?"

The creatures inside had long thought of themselves as incapable of being hurt in our reality. These beasts had never met me and this gave me the immense pleasure of introducing them to what pain really was.

"You're done 'playing' with Dr. Dyer and we don't have the time to let you play with us either. Give him to us and we will leave."

He howled again as I pressed the sword in deeper and began to twist.

The howls turned into words.

"The house!" Ammi was screaming with every voice in his head. "Dyer's in the house!"

Nancy grabbed those words with every ounce of her willpower and became a driven woman. She sprinted toward the house.

"Leo," I said. "Go with her." Leo took off after her as I held Ammi on the end of my sword.

"Please let us down, let us down!" The possessed man was shouting.

I shook my head at him. "Not until I see Dr. William Dyer inside that pickup truck."

The door to the house slammed open with a bang and out walked Nancy and Leo. Between them hung a dirt-covered old man. He was wearing a suit like what he would wear to teach class. His facial hair had become long enough to cover his neck. His hair hung to each side of his head and looked as dry and brittle as gray straw.

It was Dr. William Dyer's eyes that looked the worst. They darted around in every direction as if trying to view everything at once.

Or … possibly as if trying to avoid seeing something specific.

Dragging Dyer out, Nancy was talking to him the entire time. It wasn't audible to me, but I could tell that she was hoping to snap him out of whatever fugue he had entered.

Leo and Nancy moved past me and to the truck. As they did, Leo looked at me and nodded to Nancy. "We need to get them out of here now," he said.

I agreed wholeheartedly. Nancy's focus on her father had helped her to hold the beasts at bay, but it wouldn't last, and Dyer might already be gone. We wouldn't know for certain until we were out of the Blasted Heath.

I pulled my sword from Ammi's body, and I wasn't nice about it. At the same time, I released the spell that held him in the air. He fell with a grunt that was more Ammi than the void.

The pickup wouldn't hold four of us in the cab, so I jumped into the back and helped Leo lie Dyer down.

As Dyer's head gently touched the metal of the truck bed, I heard a menacing laugh from behind me.

I glanced over my shoulder and watched as Ammi, holding his side, laughed.

I wasn't the only person who found Ammi's laugh discomforting. Leo looked at me and asked, "What is that about?"

I looked away from Ammi and then to the path we had driven up only minutes ago. "We're too late," I replied.

"They're here."

Chapter 5: Still the Blasted Heath

The slight growl of engines and crunching of gravel could just barely be heard. They were getting closer.

I drew my .38 Smith & Wesson in my right hand and kept my left tightly gripped on the handle of my cavalry sword.

"Get into the house," I shouted. It was too late for quiet. Cultists were coming, and I had no doubts that they knew we were here. I turned to follow my companions into the shambles of a house when a solid mass slammed into the back of my knees and dragged me forcefully to the ground.

Before I landed, Ammi Pierce was already on me—slapping and clawing at me like an animal. He climbed up my waist and was tearing at my chest and face before I could get my weapons up to defend myself.

His fist, powered by something more than an old man's muscles, pumped up and down into my face. I felt my nose break and stars filled my vision. My vision cleared just enough to see Ammi Pierce raise both his hands above his head, clasp them together, and bring them down.

I twisted my neck and shoulders and managed to pull my head just barely out of the path of Ammi's clenched hands, and managed to take a glancing blow to my temple instead of the direct hit to my face. Stars shot along the right side of my vision as Ammi's knuckles brushed my skull.

My vision cleared again, and I felt Ammi shift his weight. My arms were still stuck at my sides and seemed to be held there by the willpower of whatever was wearing Ammi.

His hands were suddenly inches from my ears. As soon as I noticed that they were there, my mind was flooded with

pressure. Sound filled my mind, screams of an agony that
wasn't of this earth. Each sound was a pressure point on a place
in my mind. Every painful memory, image, or thought that I
had ever had was forcefully pushed to the front of my mind.
Each of those thoughts rode on the backs of creatures from the
void. They were tentacled, otherworldly things traveling from
Ammi Pierce and into my mind.

A piece of me realized that they weren't just coming from
Ammi, but they were the very same creatures that had chosen
Ammi for their vessel. He was filling me with his own parasites.

These creatures didn't really know Andrew Doran,
though. I had spent the better part of the last year learning to
compartmentalize my mind through living with a creature
already inside my head. These were different and not of my
own making, but the concept was similar.

That small piece of me that recognized that these creatures
were Ammi was enough of myself to gather my willpower.
While they attempted to flood my mind, they had left Ammi
wide open.

I pushed past the creatures and sent my will forward and
into Ammi's mind. With all the beasts rooting around in my
own head, Ammi's head was incredibly empty. It didn't take me
long to find what I was looking for.

The remains of Ammi's soul were tattered and barely
coherent as having once been a person. In my mind's eye, his
soul looked similar to his body, but without any specific border.
Pieces flaked off and drifted away in the emptiness of his mind.
He didn't have many years left in this state, and I wondered
what the creatures would do once they lost their plaything.

I poked Ammi with my mind, prodding him for some sort
of reaction. He had obviously been tortured for far too long, and
didn't respond to any of my pokes.

So, I punched him.

Metaphorically, of course, as my hands were still pinned to
my side, and I had no idea what was going on outside of my
mind. As I had mentioned earlier, I had been strengthening my
mind for the better part of the last year. I took that strength and
used it to make a mental punch directly at the center of Ammi's

psyche. If I had to, I would destroy him altogether, but I was hoping that it wouldn't come to that.

I was placing my bets on the fact that the creatures controlling Ammi still needed him. Otherwise they had held him for far too long to just be torturing him for fun. They needed Ammi's soul on this side of the veil to anchor them here.

My bets were spot on. I could feel the creatures retracting from my mind almost as soon as I attacked Ammi. As they returned to their mind, I returned to mine.

My consciousness flooded into my damaged body, and my eyes were no longer filled with stars. Instead, I watched as Ammi Pierce's body shuddered and rocked before sliding off me.

The creatures were struggling to regain the balance they had needed inside Ammi's head. The distraction forced them to release their power on my arms and I was suddenly free.

Bleeding and dizzy, I got to my feet as quickly as I could, moving away from Ammi while I did so. I tested my grip on my sword and pistol, flexing my fingers as I turned back toward the possessed man. Ammi shuddered again before his back straightened and his eyes were filled with the inhuman look of the creatures.

Ammi's possessed body rose to its feet. The air around it seemed to ripple with power and I heard the vehicles coming ever closer.

Gripping the sword tighter, I said through my already swollen lips, "Ammi, I don't have time for this." I ignored the blood oozing over my mouth as I continued. "Worshipers of the Serpent God, Yig, if we're lucky, are coming into *your* Heath to get William Dyer." I couldn't get a read on Ammi's thoughts, his face was alien ... impossible to read. "They will sense the power here and they will not stop at Dyer. They will want that power for themselves." There was still no response. "They will take your Colour from the Well!" I was shouting and blood was spraying from my mouth. The well was the last card I had to play.

There was a slight twitch in Ammi's brow. My words were making the creatures think. If I was correct, then they would soon be fighting the Nazi-employed cultists for me.

Ammi shouted, "They can try!" He ran at me with incredible speed. In that moment, I realized that Ammi didn't care about the Nazis or any of their followers. All he cared about was the threat in front of him and he would take care of that one and then the next one as they came.

While Ammi and the beasts within him traveled faster than I could possibly have hoped to, he didn't travel faster than it took to raise my gun.

The first bullet from my magically enhanced pistol slammed into Ammi's chest. It was a lower shot than I had intended. Ammi's heart stopped sustaining his life a long time ago. Blood didn't even blossom from the wound. A hole punched into Ammi's chest and he didn't slow in his lunge toward me.

The second bullet hit exactly where I had aimed it, cutting a hole above Ammi's left eye. It was just a black void in his head, but it had the desired effect. Otherworldly spirits or gods from another dimension, it just didn't matter. No matter what creatures were driving Ammi's body, they couldn't do it without his brain.

That didn't stop them from trying, though. Ammi Pierce's body continued to surge forward, but stumbled and lost stride. The skin around the bullet hole darkened in a decaying spiderweb pattern. The effect of the magically-propelled ammunition was different on different creatures, and it was killing the evil within Ammi in a way that I hadn't seen before.

It was as if someone had deflated Ammi, and he collapsed to the ground at my feet.

I took only a moment to reach down and check that the animating force that had been inside Ammi's body had left. I also mumbled a deeply felt, "I'm sorry," but I don't know if I was saying it to Ammi Pierce or to the person who would soon be the next vehicle of choice for the void beasts.

I didn't have much time to think on it before gunfire was exploding all around me. I spun toward where they were coming from and was facing the shack.

Leo was standing on the dilapidated porch with a pistol in each hand. In Nancy's stupor, he must have taken up her weapon. Leo was firing over and past me. I spun around again to see where the bullets were landing and watched as they punched holes into the side of one of the two trucks that were pulling up. They were two old farm pickups and I recognized them immediately. Of course, the large "Property of Miskatonic University" helped, but I also knew them as the utility trucks that were usually seen around my alma mater's student housing. These were more cultists who had been residing just a little too close to my home for me to have been comfortable.

The realization came to me that I hadn't actually ever been safe. The Nazi agents had only been biding their time until all of their pieces were in play. I wasn't Dean of that damnable University any more than I had been before Brandon Smythe's tenure.

Both trucks were loaded with eight cultists each: two in each cab and six in each bed. Each of their faces were covered in dark tattoos, with intricate runes that stretched down past their necks and onto their bare chests. Their bare chests were also covered with straps that looped over one shoulder and connected to very large guns.

They returned fire almost immediately. The Nazis people leapt from the trucks and marched forward to rain a steady stream of bullets at myself, out in the open, and the shack where my companions waited.

I dropped to a crouch as our aggressors' feet touched the dead soil of the Blasted Heath. My pains were suddenly a distant memory as I ran directly for the dilapidated shack. I didn't slow as I went up the three rotting steps, crossed the tiny porch, and dived through the doorway.

Leo continued to shoot from behind me, but backed into the shack as he did so. Once I saw him clear the threshold, I kicked out at the door from my position on the floor. It slammed shut and Leo shouted in French, "Get the table!"

I stood and the blood rushed from my head. I was dizzy and suddenly remembering the beating that I had only just received. As I regained my footing, I took in my surroundings...

...and gagged.

Animal body parts littered the barren shack. There was no furniture aside from the one large oak table. The table was covered in more animal parts and the closer I looked the more I saw how those animals had died.

Human bite marks were all over the parts, and the parts were in varying states of decay. Ammi had lived like less than an animal, eating to survive, but leaving the remains to rot in his own home.

In a (surprisingly clean) corner of the shack lay William Dyer with his head on the lap of his daughter. Nancy held her father tightly and continued to mumble whatever she had been mumbling to him earlier. It sounded like a children's story this time.

William Dyer's eyes were wide open, but he wasn't looking at anything in this world.

I found my feet quickly enough and Leo and I ignored the carrion on the table as we lifted the heavy beast, flipped it, and slammed the top against the door for added support. To our fortune, bullets slammed into the door at that moment, but didn't pass through the table. Not yet, anyway.

I crouched behind the table with Leo and reloaded my .38 Smith and Wesson from the ammunition I kept in my holster belt. I realized that I was still tightly gripping my sword and slid it back into its sheath at my side. Leo was emptying one of the pistols and using the remainder of the bullets to reload the other. We were pitiful adversaries and it wouldn't take our attackers long to realize it.

I waved my pistol in the direction of the Dyer family. "Only us, then?" Leo only nodded and I noticed the stress behind his eyes wasn't entirely in response to our newest Nazi-employed attackers.

The Blasted Heath was still pressing on his mind, and probably more so since I had killed Ammi Pierce. Leo had seen that and I hoped he hadn't seen it as an act of betrayal.

I nodded toward the door. "I'm sorry that I killed him."

Leo shook his head and only spoke in French, it was easier. "No. It was either you or him. You made the right choice." He forced a smile and looked away from his reloaded pistol, tossing the other one into some animal parts that resembled something like a pig. "Besides, one of those men out there has to be more weak-willed than I."

I nodded to my friend. "Any ideas?"

Leo shrugged. "I shoot people. Ideas are your thing." He forced himself to say it in English.

I returned Leo's shrug. "Well, I'm all out."

Leo was about to make some sort of suggestion that I was certain ended with the words "blaze of glory," when a new voice joined the conversation.

"Hold your fire!" The voice echoed outside of the shack. It sounded like it was coming from just at the end of the rotten steps.

"Dr. Doran," he lowered his shouting, but we could still hear him well enough. "You know why we are here. Send out the geologist and we will be on our way."

His voice was deep and solid. This man was confident, but there was something else behind his voice. He sounded tired, beaten, even though he had us over the fire.

Barking a laugh, I replied, "I'm supposed to believe that? You will let us go, completely unharmed?" I laughed again.

"Today, yes!" He shouted and it was almost a sigh. "This chase, the body count, it's all too much. You're bringing unwanted attention to our actions. So, today we will give you a pass. Give us the geologist and we will be on our way. No harm, no foul." There was a pause. "You have my word."

Leo joined me with a laugh then. "The word of a Cthulhu Cultist? What? Did the Nazis run out of Yig followers?"

Leo tilted his head to the side and eyed me with a hint of a smile. "You did ask for a better quality of cultist."

I frowned at him, hissing, "Shut up!"

"Dr. Doran, be reasonable. I am not your enemy. I am only not your friend. I don't like the Nazis any more than you do, heck, I'm an American from Rutland, Vermont." Rutland's foremost expert in Cthulhu paused, probably hoping to give me time to absorb his red-blooded American status. "We have mutual needs. The Nazis want the geologist, and so do my friends. Knowing that, I am putting all of my chips on the Nazis being in over their heads. I just want to be there to pick up the pieces."

I nodded to no one in particular and replied, "In that, we're in agreement. The Nazis have no idea what they are getting into by hiring a bunch of backstabbing cultists to do their stateside work." Snapping my fingers, I motioned for Leo to stay low and check the back. This was a lot of chit chat for someone who seemed to know a thing or two about me.

"The city in the south," Rutland continued, "is a powder keg. The wick has already been lit. Give me the geologist and I'll watch—hell, I'll even take pictures for you, Doctor—as the Nazis destroy themselves."

"Thank you for thinking of me, Rutland. That's very considerate of you." I tightened my grip on the .38 and slid further back from the table. "Unfortunately, I think that you have misread me. I hate you monster-worshiping cultists more than I hate the Nazis. I don't need Cthulhu's lackeys ushering in the new world order any more than I want the Nazis to do it."

A crash alerted me to a struggle in the back of the house. Leo had just stepped out of the back door and the sound was just outside. There were two gunshots before Leo came back inside, slamming the door, carrying a machine gun and with a rifle slung over his shoulder.

Rutland spoke up as soon as Leo was back inside Ammi Pierce's shack. "Please remember that I tried to end this differently, Dr. Doran."

A hum filled the air around us and the whole world seemed to heave with an unseen force. The walls shook around us, dust and dirt fell from the ceiling, covering us each with the debris from the old house.

The walls were shuddering the worst and as Leo and I spun, trying to discover the source of the tremor, our eyes fell upon Nancy and William as they sat there ignoring the house falling apart around them.

"Nancy, get away from the wall!" I shouted over the hum and the rattling of the walls.

Wherever Nancy was, she wasn't capable of hearing anything in this world. Leo ran forward and grabbed the prone girl by the ankle and her father by his wrist. A quick tug through the effluence of deceased animals and the Dyer family was safe from the rattling walls.

Leo came back to me, a dutiful soldier awaiting orders. "Is the back clear?" I asked him.

He hefted the machine gun and turned toward the back door. "It will be."

That left me with the issue of the catatonic William Dyer and his quickly fading daughter. I moved to Dyer and flipped him over. His face had a smear of something on it that I couldn't identify. Lifting his chin, I pulled open his eyelids and looked into them.

With my trained eye, an eye well versed in the poisons that leak from one world and into the next, I could see that this wasn't some sort of medically related issue. William Dyer simply wasn't in his body at all.

When a person leaves their body, it is almost never entirely. When I went to the Dream Lands, or when a person or being possesses another entity, they have to leave a trail of themselves behind or they will never find their way back. It's never much, and usually the traveler is unaware that a piece has been left, but unless purposefully severed, that link is always there.

I could see, only barely, that small link between William Dyer's body and his consciousness. He was elsewhere, but he still might be able to find his way back.

With help.

I slapped him hard across the face. I doubted that it would help, but Dyer had been the source of much of my recent heartache. It helped me.

Touching the power of the void, I shouted over the hum that was tearing down the entire shack around us.

"Your daughter is in danger, William! She will die if you don't get up and follow us out of here right now!"

A thunderous crack filled the air and I dropped the geologist as I slapped my hands over my ears. Spinning around, I watched as outside light appeared at the base of each of the walls. The cultists were lifting the house off its foundation.

I spun back to the Dyers, completely prepared to die as I

dragged them both from the remains of the shack.

Instead, I was greeted by the standing and very healthy looking form of Dr. William Dyer as he scooped up his daughter in his arms and looked me directly in the eyes.

"I don't have much time, Andrew. I suggest that we move now." His voice was dry and raspy, yet strong and full of life.

I wasn't about to argue, and instead ran ahead of him toward the back door. As I put my hand on the door, machine gun fire stopped me from pushing it open. Dyer and I flinched, dropping into a half-crouch before realizing that it wasn't aimed at us.

Raising my pistol, just in case, I kicked open the back door and stepped outside. To the left of the back door of the shack, Leo was firing wildly into a group of the Cthulhu cultists. I did a quick scan to my right and was just in time to see several more cultists trying to flank my friend.

Firing two shots, I stopped them in their tracks and their momentum carried them forward, face-first into the dead soil that was the trademark of the Blasted Heath.

"Head into the woods." I told them, but it was obvious that they couldn't head back to the truck. William took his daughter and ran straight away from the house and into the wilted forest. The vegetation was dead and dry, but it was better cover than standing still.

I followed them as Leo covered our exit with more gun fire. We made our way swiftly through the forest, and the farther that we got from the shack, the more the vegetation seemed to be growing at least marginally healthier.

William had no idea where he was going, but I let him lead anyway. 'Away' was as good an idea as I could come up with, and the geologist was definitely heading 'away.' Doing my best to keep an eye on the Dyers and Leo, I continued to spin as I ran after them, firing behind me and then looking forward.

I reloaded twice before Leo's borrowed machine gun began to click. His ammunition was out. He tossed the weapon away, and in the same smooth motion swung the rifle from his shoulder and took aim.

I had noticed much earlier in this fight that my mind wasn't immune to the effects of the pressure that the creature of the

Heath had put on it. My concentration was impossible to focus, and it had been damaging my aim. The first shot on Ammi hadn't been meant to hit his chest and I had gotten lucky when I came out of the back door. So, as we moved through the woods, it wasn't the thickening foliage that alerted me to the lessened effects of the thing in the well so much as my steadily increasing aim.

I had been beaten, bloodied, shot at, and chased, and I was tired. Instead of my shots missing even more and more than they had been, which would have been expected, my shots were actually finding their marks more frequently. The influence of the weakened veil was fading.

I was beginning to think that we might actually make it out of there.

Thud.

William collapsed ahead of me. We were moving with such speed that I almost tripped over the prone bodies of him and his daughter. I hopped and skidded to a halt.

Dropping to Dyer's side, I saw that he was still with us. Leo caught up quickly and crouched, taking up a defensive position.

"I can't hold … I can't hold on any longer." William sounded weak and distant. "Save her, Andrew!"

I grabbed the fading old man by the collar. "How do I save you?" I demanded. "I need you!"

William's eyes cast about looking, but not seeing. "The Peasley expedition to Australia." He was babbling at that point. "There are tricks to time, Andrew." His face took on a smile that would have looked more at place on the face of a youngster who had learned a secret that he couldn't tell. "You have already saved me, you only need to catch up."

The sounds of the cultists making their way through the woods were getting louder. Our time had run out.

"Nancy, what are you doing?" Dyer suddenly demanded. Stress had flooded his face and he looked terrified. "Put down the gun, my girl!" He sounded like he was trying to talk down his daughter, but I could see that she wasn't doing anything worth talking down. She was still unconscious in the dirt.

Just as suddenly as his outburst, William's face was suddenly lax and his eyes were as empty as they had been in the shack.

Leo had stopped shooting during William's sudden excitement, but in that time the cultists had gotten much closer. He looked at me and stated, very calmly, "We could use a way out of this."

He raised his gun to fire, but I reached up and grabbed his arm, stopping him. I looked at Nancy and William, trying to formulate some plan that could help us.

William was back to his original state and was completely useless. His daughter was beginning to stir, but she might as well have been just as far away as her father was. They would be of no help.

That was when I began mumbling to myself. "Out ... out ... we need a way ... out..." Leo probably thought that I had finally lost my mind, but I recovered just as quickly. I slapped his gun arm, "I have an idea!"

I dragged William's body closer to that of his daughter and grabbed one of their hands in each of mine. I nodded toward my hand and said, "Grab Nancy and William's other hands. Quickly."

Leo didn't like that. "If I hold their hands, I will not be able to hold the gun." I nodded, but I didn't say anything. Grunting, Leo did as I asked. He swung the rifle around and allowed it to rest on its strap over his shoulder. Just as quickly, he scooped up each of the Dyer's remaining hands and asked, "Now what?"

I gave him a very serious look and he seemed to take it that way despite my broken nose, black eyes, and blood-covered mouth and chin. "Don't move or let go, no matter what you see or hear."

I began chanting.

The chanting wasn't completely necessary, but it helped. Magic, at least the way that I had learned to use it, was a matter of borrowing the forces that leaked through the veil and applying them to our world. Concentrating on saying an incantation or chant helped keep your mind rooted in forming those energies into the shape that you wished. It could be done without the chanting to guide it, but that route required a lot more concentration than my broken face was capable of at that time.

I felt the power surge through me. The veil was still weak

that close to the Heath and the power came so easily. It had to. Normally, the spell I was attempting would have required too much energy for me to succeed at it. The result would have been either an unconscious Andrew Doran or an Andrew Doran whose soul had lit on fire and consumed him from the inside.

The concept of what I was trying to do, though, was incredibly simple. There is a reason that I refer to the space between the two realities a 'veil.' The term veil is the best word that I could come up with that fully encapsulates and simplifies the physics of the membrane between our universe and the void.

What I was about to do was pick up the edge of that veil and drape it over us. The result would be to shift us just barely out of our home reality and completely out of detection from the cultists.

Even with the power boost that I was feeling so close to the void, the strain was unbearable. I could feel the forces of the Universe coursing through me and pressing out of me. I felt about ready to explode. I couldn't release it, though. Even if the void were to consume me, Leo could complete the task of stopping the Germans from getting any of the alien weapons.

I kept my eyes open through the strain, needing to see if the magic was taking effect. The air around and between us shimmered with a much more visible version of that almost purple light I'd seen previously. Past the orb of color that surrounded us, the rest of the world began to turn transparent. The ground, the trees, the rocks, and everything of the reality that we were leaving behind became part a reality that we were not. The only solid item of our new-found reality was the group of us within the bubble I was making.

Terror crossed Leo's eyes and I spared a quick glance in the direction that he was looking. The cultists had caught up with us. My little magic trick was about to be put to the test. I was hoping that I could hold out long enough for them to get by.

It wasn't Rutland's entire band of merry cultists, but it was most of them. I didn't take the time to count, but I could tell that a few of the remaining troops were hanging back at the shack in case we circled back.

They passed through us as if we weren't even there. We

were spirits in the forest of the Blasted Heath. We were removed enough to still see what was going on, but we weren't in our home reality anymore. In effect, I had turned us into the same creatures that had inhabited Ammi's body. There was a slight chance that they might come and find us in this vulnerable state, but I didn't plan on us being under the veil long enough to find out.

The cultists slowed as they went through us, not because of any sense of our presence, but because we had made a lot of noise somewhere near this place. I could tell that they were looking for signs of where we had gone. One in particular, who I assumed had to be Rutland, circled the clearing that we were in. He stopped when he was standing directly in the same spot that I was.

He must have seen the depression where I had knelt to grab the Dyers' hands, but without me there, he had no idea where I could have gone.

Rutland pointed at two of the cultists. "Go east 500 yards and then circle back to the shack." He waved his hand around to indicate the rest of the group of cultists. "Move out." The two that he had indicated branched off left from the direction that we had previously headed, while the rest of the cultists continued with Rutland in the same direction that we had headed.

Once I couldn't hear the cultists anymore, I released the Dyer family's hands. The world snapped back into focus and I sagged with exhaustion. I had no time to be tired, though. It wouldn't take long for the two groups to realize that they lost us and circle back. We had to move.

I forced myself to my feet and grabbed Nancy's wrist. She was groggy still, but she had come back to herself enough that I could drag her to her feet. Hopefully, she would stay standing long enough to get out of this mess.

"Truck," I said through an exhausted and blood covered mouth. "We have to get back to the truck." I didn't let go of Nancy's hand as Leo scooped up William and threw him over his shoulder. With his other arm, he shrugged off the rifle and held the grip in one hand. We started back toward the shack with as much hustle as we could muster.

We got back to the shack without any issues, but Leo stopped us at the edge of the woods. He set Dyer down and put a proper grip on the rifle, letting the strap hang down.

"Wait for me here," he said.

Leo ran out and around the shack while Nancy and I sat crouched around her father. I looked at her eyes and saw that the increased proximity to the center of the Blasted Heath was already pressing on her mind. I had felt it as well, but I could see her falling back into her stupor.

My examination of my newest companion ended almost as soon as it started. Two rapid gunshots echoed and snapped me to attention. Silence followed, and in it I knew our position had just been given away to the rest of the cultists. I had no doubts that they were returning to the shack as quickly as their feet could carry them.

Leo came around the shack the same way that he had left. The rifle was already slung over his shoulder as he scooped up William and said to me, "We must hurry."

I had never let go of Nancy's hand, and pulled her with me in the wake of Leo and her father. We ran around the house. In front of the porch were two dead Cthulhu cultists lying in the dust of the front yard only a few feet from their weapons.

A quick glance showed me that Leo had also slashed the tires of Rutland's trucks.

We got to Leo's truck quickly and jumped in. Leo deposited William in the bed of the truck while I slid Nancy into the passenger seat of the cab. Closing the truck bed, I climbed up the back and swung my leg in while Leo tossed me his rifle and hopped behind the steering wheel.

I almost lost my footing as Leo put the truck into gear and took off. I grabbed the edge of the truck bed. His tires spun on the gravel with such force that I almost didn't notice the cultists coming around the house. As the cultists started firing, I crouched low to keep upright in the truck bed and tried to take aim with Leo's rifle.

I managed to get three poorly aimed shots off before Leo carried us out of sight of Rutland's cultists.

Chapter 6: Innsmouth

Leo took the pickup truck down winding back roads for miles until even I had no idea where in Massachusetts we were. Once I was sure that the cultists weren't going to find us any time soon, I knocked on the rear window of Leo's truck and yelled for him to stop.

The truck slid to a slow stop on the gravel as Leo took into account that William and myself were still loose cargo in the bed of the truck. I was glad he did.

The adrenaline from the battle in the Blasted Heath had left my system and I was crashing hard. My face was puffy and raw and breathing was something that I was only willing to do through my mouth. My eyes felt as puffy as the rest of my face, and vision was beginning to disappear from my right eye as it swelled shut.

Aside from the pain to my face, I was exhausted. The running, the carrying, the magic, the adrenaline, all of it came to a head and crashed down on me. It was everything that I could do to not collapse altogether, but we weren't safe yet.

I slowly climbed from the back of the truck while Leo and Nancy climbed down from the cab and met me at the tailgate.

They both flinched when they saw my face. I did the best that I could not to register their reactions.

"What do we do now?" Leo asked.

I shook my head. "We can't go back to Miskatonic University."

Nancy, who had seemingly recovered from her time in the Blasted Heath, asked, "Why not?"

"It's been compromised," I answered. "The trucks they were driving were Miskatonic Utility trucks. The Yig cultists that stormed my office were dressed as students. They've been watching us for months, maybe longer, and now that they know that we know they are there, it's the least safe place for us."

"What were they waiting for?" Nancy asked.

I looked to the back of the truck and then to Nancy. "Well, I think they were waiting for your father, but when you showed up they didn't want to lose the chance that you presented for them."

Leo asked, "How are we supposed to mount a global expedition without the resources of the school?"

I tried to smile, but it hurt too much. Instead, I said, "Not all the school's resources are lost to us."

"What does that mean?" Nancy asked.

I ignored her and asked, "How are you feeling?"

Nancy's face was about as pale as mine was purple, and it paled further as my question reminded her about her time in the Blasted Heath.

"Invaded. Violated," she took a deep breath. "I'm trying to move on from it."

I nodded. It was the only answer that my exhausted mind could give her. She would recover, but she would never be the same. Her identity had been compromised. There was nothing as privately yours as the thoughts in your head, and Nancy had seen those compromised by creatures as vile and alien as they came.

So, I went ahead and answered Nancy's original question. "Miskatonic University's history is filled with darkness, and not just that locked up Necronomicon. Arkham has always been a home, or a focus, for the darker forces of the void. When the school was built, it became a natural magnet for all of those forces and over the years, time and time again, bad things happen. In response to this, about thirty or so years ago, some of the staff got together and put contingency plans in place. Armitage, Halsey, Lake, they all made a decision: In the event that the school would be inaccessible, there would be contingencies in place that would facilitate the return of the status quo. The only person who would have complete access to that information would be the Dean, selected by the board."

Leo smiled. "They made a battle plan for taking back the school."

"Among other things," I answered. "The plan was only a small part of it. It was more than likely that such an event would destroy the school, so resources were squirrelled away by the different Deans over the years to aid in rebuilding, if that were the case. All of these details were locked away in a safe within the … armory." I hesitated mentioning the secrets of the University, such as the armory, in front of Nancy. In the end, I decided that it didn't matter. She was in the deep end of it now, it made no sense trying to protect her from that tidbit of information.

Nancy didn't even care about the mentioning of the armory. She was frowning. "That's all well and good, but these plans don't do us any good locked away on the very same campus that we can't return to."

"Well, I don't like secrets that are shared, especially given the history of the school, but I did like the idea of a contingency plan." I tried again to smile before remembering that my face was very much against that idea. I hissed with the pain before continuing. "I started hiding away my own resources the moment that the board gave me the position of Dean. These resources are ours for the taking, and they include one of Miskatonic University's large boats."

"Where?" Leo begs.

"Not far," I replied. "Innsmouth."

I gave Leo the directions to Innsmouth, Massachusetts from Arkham and we hopped back into the truck. I laid down next to William's unconscious body in the bed of the truck and did my best to rest. Innsmouth was about ten miles from Arkham. Leo would find his way back to a main road and then head in that direction.

Despite the bumpy roads and the lack of security in the back of the truck, I managed to fall asleep.

When I woke up, it was to the sound of the truck doors slamming shut. I sat up and looked around. Night had fallen. I leaned over to check on William. He was still alive, but not really there.

I climbed out using the tire well and joined my companions at the front of the truck. Before the truck was a large fence made from a mix of sheets of metal and planks of wood. It stood at least twice the height of the truck and was covered in signs that read:

No Trespassing!
Keep Out!
and
By Order of the Federal Bureau of Investigations
This Area is Off Limits to All Unauthorized Personnel.

Leo waved at the nearest of the signs and asked, "What the hell is all of this about?"

I took a deep breath, noticed a pain in my ribs and wondered when that had happened. After my brief hesitation, I explained Innsmouth, Massachusetts.

"At the turn of the century, Innsmouth was home to a very secluded cult. They closed their doors to outsiders and spent their nights in reverence of their deity, Dagon. Except Dagon wasn't actually a deity so much as he was a water-dwelling creature of the void. He had found a home in the nearby Devil's Reef and had provided gold and riches to his worshipers. Devil's Reef is just off the coast of Innsmouth. In exchange for those riches they had to ... mate ... with his children."

Leo grimaced but he didn't interrupt me. Nancy's face remained attentive but unreadable.

"The interbreeding created a culture of half-fish/half-men that continued the process well into the 1920s. In 1928, the FBI learned of the creatures that had become the dominant species in Innsmouth and raided the port city. They killed as many of the creatures as they could and drove the rest back to their home at Devil's Reef. Once the FBI had pushed them all to the Reef, they bombed it, killing most of them."

"Most of them?" Nancy asked.

"I ran into a few of them about a year back. They had a piece of the reef with them and were looking to start over in Barcelona. I stopped them."

"If they are dead, then why the fence?" Leo asked.

"The FBI are never happy with just bombing something, they wanted to make sure no one would ever come back. That's why I chose it. When I had discovered the fence, I began funneling Miskatonic resources here and mobilizing the locals."

"Locals?" Nancy asked. "I thought you said that the FBI forced everyone out."

"They tried," I replied. "Some of them managed to hide."

Leo gulped. "More fishpeople?"

"Kind of," I said. "Not quite."

"More monsters." Leo sounded annoyed. He unclipped the magazine from the rifle and held it up for me to examine. It was empty. "We're in no position to fight."

I placed my hand on Leo's shoulder and looked him in the eyes with my one good eye. "I am certain that we won't have to." I waved at the truck. "Get back into the truck, I'll open the way."

There was no visible door in the fence and I was surprised at first that neither Nancy nor Leo asked what I meant by opening a way. My surprise vanished when I realized how tired I felt even after my light sleep in the pickup. They were having just as hard a day as I was.

I approached the wall directly in front of the truck and barked out some words from the Necronomicon. They had no meaning in the order that I had strung them together, but they worked to deactivate the magical locks I had put in place over the wall.

There was a loud grating sound and the section of the fence I had spoken to shuddered before sliding back about a foot and then sliding out of the way and to the left. The road into Innsmouth was cleared.

I waved the truck through and walked alongside it as Leo drove into the ruins of the town formerly known as Innsmouth.

I had never seen Innsmouth before the federal raid of the city, but I had to hope that it had been better than what was greeting Leo and Nancy as they entered. The city had a grime to it that almost seemed alive. The walls that still stood were covered in a mix of moss and slime, as if the city itself had been buried at the bottom of a deep lagoon, only to resurface a few hours before we arrived.

There were no windows in any of the surviving buildings. Not even broken pieces of glass had survived. The windows were all completely empty frames. It was as if we were looking at the corpses of a battle field. The buildings had died in an intense battle, and now their empty, dead eyes stared at us.

The road had been an antique stone road and the years had been no nicer to it. Where the stones were still in the road, they were uneven and broken. I felt sorry for Nancy's father in the back of the truck.

Where the grease and slime met the decay and detritus of a city already dead for decades, there was some life. In the corners and on small plots of earth that seemed out of place, grass and vines grew. It was a losing battle, but a battle that the earth still hadn't given up on fighting.

One of the collapsed buildings, specifically the tower from what looked like it had once been a church, had fallen into the road, forcing Leo to stop the truck.

"We walk from here," I said.

Nancy and Leo climbed down from the truck and came over to me.

"What about my father?" Nancy asked. "I am not leaving him here." As she said it, she glanced around her. The decayed look of the city was giving her an odd feeling. She was fearing another intrusion on her mind. I didn't know how to convince her that she was safe, so I didn't even try.

"My friends will take care of him." I answered.

Stress crossed Leo's face as fear danced across Nancy's. They knew that I had allies in this city, but they hadn't yet settled on the idea that they could meet them. Meeting fishpeople had that effect on everyone.

"Your friends?" Leo asked, casting his eyes about.

I raised my voice. "You can come out now."

Across what had once been the central square of Innsmouth, around thirty people climbed from the rubble or from behind dilapidated vehicles. Their ages ranged from Nancy's early years to old age, with no children in the mix.

Thirty very normal looking people.

"But..." Nancy started and then stopped for a moment before continuing. "They look normal. I thought that they were fishpeople."

I nodded. "In the eyes of Dagon and his children, they are mutations and birth defects. To us, they're just people. They are outcasts among the monsters and monsters among civilization. Ostracized by both." I smiled at Nancy and didn't care how much pain it sent through my face. "They're like us."

"Allies," the French rebel added. I agreed with him.

"Why do they live here?" Nancy asked.

I looked at our approaching welcome party as I answered. "When the FBI took to bombing the Reef and planting explosives in the town, any survivors who couldn't be pushed into the sea were gathered and taken to government facilities. Concentration camps with laboratories for studying the anomalies of these people." I sighed. "The Innsmouth people who could complete their change into fishpeople and flee to the sea did, leaving behind those who couldn't. The fishpeople who couldn't change quite so quickly became a priority to the FBI and they scrambled to get them first." I waved at the group still approaching. "That gave our friends here some time to hide. Fear from being found out stops them from ever leaving. Until I found them, they were barely surviving. A percentage of the supplies that I ferret away goes toward helping the survivors of Innsmouth. In exchange, they keep my secret."

"He's modest," barked an older and grizzly looking gentleman who was approaching. "Andrew Doran saved our lives."

The man had a white beard and no hair on his head. His clothes consisted of dark pants and a white shirt, all covered by a navy blue coat. He hugged Nancy and then pumped Leo's hand with both of his. "Friends of Andrew are family to us."

He stepped back from his greeting and his people gathered to a halt behind him. "My name is Sebastian Eliot. I am the Pastor and leader for the survivors. Welcome to Innsmouth."

"We have a man who needs care in the back of the truck." I said.

Sebastian responded by directing some of his people toward the truck. He then began guiding us with him toward one of the collapsed buildings. We stepped through a door frame that long ago fell apart. It had become more of a door ... hole. It was dark, but Sebastian guided us gently, keeping us from tripping as we moved further toward the back of the destroyed architecture.

"We were able to survive the attack from the FBI because Innsmouth is riddled with tunnels. Our more aquatic kin aren't fans of the daylight, and the town's benefactor, Obed Marsh, had the tunnels built to connect every building in Innsmouth." We came to a fireplace that I could only barely make out in the non-existent lighting. He kicked something to the left of it and the fireplace slid away. "We have lived down here since."

"There were other survivors though, weren't there? Andrew said that he ran into a few on a trip to Barcelona." Nancy was genuinely curious as she followed us down the steps that had opened up behind the fireplace.

"Well," Sebastian started, "Innsmouth was hardly the last bastion of Dagon's will, but it sounds to me as though Andrew's Barcelona fishpeople were one of the four tribes."

A flash of confusion and then anger came over me. "What do you mean 'four tribes?'"

The stairwell opened to a well-lit tunnel made of brick. The lighting was spaced overhead about ten feet with every light. Somehow, my allies in Innsmouth had managed to tap into the electrical grid since the last time I had been by.

Sebastian glanced at me over his shoulder as he continued to lead us through the tunnel.

"We weren't the only survivors, but you already know that. When the bombs destroyed the Devil's Reef, there were cousins of mine who wanted to rebuild. They gathered the largest pieces, of which there were four."

The revelation of there being more pieces of the Reef that had survived sent an almost physical pang up my spine.

Sebastian continued. "Our surviving cousins divided into four different groups and went in search of new homes across the globe. America was no longer safe for them, but that didn't mean that other countries wouldn't be more ... hospitable."

Annoyance filled my soul as I begged, "Where? Where did they all go?"

Sebastian stopped walking and turned to face me, sympathy in his eyes. "They betrayed us and cast us out because we were less than what they wanted us to be. We were too human. You came here and you saved us from a meaningless existence." He gave me a sad smile. "I would tell you if I knew, but until you mentioned Barcelona, I had no idea. They didn't trust us and were afraid we would tell the FBI if they ever captured one of us." He clasped my shoulder. "If anyone can find them, it will be you, old friend."

I smiled to hide how annoyed I still felt. It wasn't Sebastian's fault that these creatures were out in the world spreading their corrupting influence. It wasn't Sebastian's fault that man is a greedy beast who will do anything in his power for another gold trinket from the sea.

Leo tapped my arm, drawing my attention. "It looks as though we have more work ahead of us." The French soldier was smiling. I nodded, but let the matter drop.

Sebastian resumed the march through the well-lit tunnels for another minute or two before the hall opened into a large underground room. It was a warehouse without windows that was at least a hundred yards long and half of that as wide. Aside from the underground aspect, the entire warehouse seemed like every other that I had ever been in, except that all the crates and boxes were labeled with the stamp of "Property of Miskatonic University."

"Doesn't it bother you," asked Nancy, "stealing from your place of employment?"

I laughed and a shot of pain went through my face and my shut eye. "Let me tell you about my place of employment," I said. "Miskatonic University disavowed any knowledge of my existence for almost a decade. Then, after I had finally decided that they were the enemy, they forced me into helping them pull their asses from the fire." I took a deep breath, not realizing how much of this had really bothered me until Nancy's snide comment. "Once I thought myself free of their plots and evil-doings, the Board of Directors voted that I be in charge of the damned place, completely forgetting our shared years of mutual loathing."

Nancy frowned. "Why did you accept the job?"

I gave her a very stern look with my one good eye. "I would rather be the gatekeeper of Hell than one of the people it steps on." I gave a small laugh, "Besides, how could I have stolen all of this without their help?"

I caught Nancy roll her eyes before she asked, "And what about the ship? We're not going to build it from the crates, are we?"

Sebastian hopped up onto one of the crates, swinging his legs as he sat. It was surprisingly limber for how aged the man appeared. "The FBI has become a steady presence in our lives. They do regular checkups on the fence and sometimes we see a patrol in the water. Fortunately, they've become very predictable as well." He waved his hand in the air, indicating outside. "The boat stays in the harbor until the week that we predict the FBI to show up. Then we take it for a small voyage." He looked from Nancy to me. "It will return by tomorrow morning."

I clapped my hands together loudly. "Great! That gives us just enough time to get some sleep and get our supplies to the dock." I turned to Nancy. "Except for you. Once you're well-rested, I need you working on translating that journal."

She nodded and then asked, "What about my father?"

Sebastian hopped down from the crate he was sitting on. "I will be attempting to bring him back to us. I promise you that I will do my best."

This seemed to placate Nancy. We allowed one of Sebastian's people to lead us to our temporary rooms. Sleep was much needed.

When I awoke, I was impressed by how sore my body was. It was as if I had been beaten during my sleep as well as during the previous day. My eye was still swollen, but Sebastian had given me some salve he had made to rub on it. The swelling had gone down and I could see out of it. The pain countered the pleasure of having my vision back. I contemplated even getting up, but the world wasn't about to save itself. I sat up.

After the initial struggle from the cot, I realized that, aside from the pain coursing through my body, I felt very well-rested.

My sleep had been uninterrupted by dreams or anything else. It was an incredibly peaceful sleep and I was suspicious.

When I had excised Olivia from my mind, what had I cut out with her? Was my ability to dream tied into Olivia? Did I lose some of my touch to the magic of the void? Would I even be able to recognize what had gone with her?

Either way, if giving Olivia away meant that I would sleep peacefully for the rest of my days, then I was only upset that I hadn't done it sooner.

I stood slowly and flexed and stretched, loosening up my tight muscles. Once I was capable of walking without grunting loudly, I made my way to the room that Sebastian was using to work on William.

Sebastian had collapsed and was draped over William's body. My first thought was that he had been attacked. I ran over, ignoring the scream from my body, and jerked him up.

When I looked into his eyes, I noticed how vacant they were. He wasn't dead, but he wasn't exactly in his own body either. I snapped my fingers, calling his name gently as I did. Within moments, his eyes were fluttering open and he had rejoined me.

"I am sorry for worrying you," Sebastian said after I had explained why I was gripping his arm so tightly. "I had cast myself into Dr. Dyer's mind, searching for a piece of him that I could latch onto. It left me absent of my own body."

I understood what he meant once he explained himself. As incredible as the world of magic was, it couldn't necessarily put one person in two places. If Sebastian was going to locate William Dyer, he was going to have to leave his body to do so. The previous day's events had lead me to conclusions. I said as much to Sebastian and he smiled, understanding.

"Have you had any luck with Dyer?" I asked.

Sebastian shrugged. "That depends completely on what you already knew." He waved at William's body on the cot. "Your friend isn't ill, he simply is not there. Dr. Dyer has vacated his body and fled to some other locale."

I nodded. "That's the same conclusion that I came to. I could feel his anchor to his body, but that was it."

"The anchor is the only reason that I think that he could still come back, but it could be decades from now," Sebastian said.

I shook my head. "No, I think it will be soon. He came back to us once, but he was from another time. I think so, anyway. He said I would find him."

Sebastian raised an eyebrow at me. "You travel in odd circles, Andrew."

"You don't know the half of it," I replied.

"Either way," Sebastian continued, "he left of his own free will. I'm certain of that, and I'm almost equally certain that he can't return any other way than how he left. He has to want to come back from wherever he is."

"Well," I said, "I'm running out of patience."

Sebastian's look took on a more thoughtful nature. "What do you expect to find on this expedition of yours?"

"It doesn't matter," I answered almost too quickly. "Whatever it is that we find needs to be destroyed. I can't let the Nazis ... I can't let anyone find the things that might be there." I sighed. "Aside from what they could do with the technology, what about the other side of that equation? Dyer wrote about creatures still alive there." I paused to let that sink in. "What if that city that he found is the next beachhead for an invasion? The world can't handle a war of that scale."

Sebastian nodded. "If you're just going to destroy the city, then why all of this work to translate his journal?"

"The journal..." I started. "The moment that I knew it existed, I had to ask myself, 'What was so important that Dr. William Dyer didn't want to include it in his tell-all warning to avoid the city?'"

"What makes you think that the journal has anything to do with that vile city in the south?" Sebastian's insight was impressive, and I worried that I was being psychoanalyzed.

"For one," I answered, "the Germans want it. That's a rather dead give-away. Also, it's written using symbols from the Necronomicon."

Sebastian knew of the book. It was the same book that had helped speed along the transition of his hometown into what it was today. "You're avoiding the original question. Even if the journal is filled with secrets of the city, shouldn't you go ahead and destroy it along with the city? Why translate it?"

I ticked off the reasons on my fingers, rather sarcastically. "It can warn us of traps, prepare us for the city's defenses, warn us of the creatures we might be up against, warn us that destroying the city could destroy the world, or one of a million things that even I, with my vast experience with the world's horrors, can't imagine."

Sebastian gave me a soft smile. "All of those are great reasons, but I hardly think that any of them are *your* reason."

I returned the smile, knowing that he was correct. "I just need to know," I said. "The world is not ever going to be ready for the darkness that rests in the mountains of that Antarctica city, but I am driven to know every dark secret that the world holds." I sighed heavily.

Sebastian nodded, accepting what I was saying as the actual truth. "Your dark curiosity drives you to know more." He leaned against the cot that William Dyer rested on. "No one has ever come back from that quest."

He was right, of course. On more than one occasion that curiosity has almost destroyed me. "No, they don't." I answered. "I can't count the number of times that I have come so close to falling over the edge. I think that the only thing that has kept me safe is that my intense curiosity is tempered by an equally intense need to keep the world safe."

Sebastian barked a laugh and I jumped, startled. "No, Andrew. The fact that you think you're in any way different from the thousands who have fallen to the monsters of our world is the delusion that unites you with them." He waved his hand, dismissing the conversation. "It doesn't matter. I just wanted to hear you speak the truth of why you're doing this. I don't think you'll actually die, not soon anyway. The only thing more powerful than your suicidal curiosity is your ability to beat the odds."

I laughed with him, trying to ignore the painful truths in our discussion. It was at that moment that we were interrupted by Nancy entering.

Nancy was holding the journal, but she walked past Sebastian and me, instead walking straight to her father's side. She gently placed her hand in his, squeezing it. I moved quietly, hoping to leave her alone with her father, when she stopped me with a hand on my arm.

"I actually came to see you." She lifted the journal. "I have translated all that I could, but it wasn't much. My father used symbols and wordings that I couldn't translate or transliterate." She sighed, tilting her head to the side. It was an action that reminded me of how young she was. "The small parts that I could translate were just rewrites of the pieces that we already know. Except..."

Nancy's hesitation drew my attention. "Except what?"

"I was able to translate one other thing." She replied slowly. "Father scribbled words and symbols all over the margins throughout the journal."

"What did it say?" I was getting more impatient by the second.

"It read, 'It will devour the world,' over and over again. It just repeats it."

Sebastian took on a morose look. "That does not bode well."

I barked a laugh. "Well, that's kind of obvious." I returned my attention to Nancy. "Was there anything else that you could find?"

She shook her head.

I slammed my fist onto the edge of the cot that held her father. I was quickly learning that having one of the Dyers at my disposal wasn't the same as having the correct Dyer at my disposal. "Then we have even more need to wake your father sooner rather than later."

Nancy's brow furrowed and I was worried that my remark on the urgency of waking her father was about to be chastised. To my surprise, she instead said, "Leo mentioned that father woke up while we were in the Blasted Heath. How did you accomplish that?"

I frowned as I thought back on it. "Yes and no. Your father woke up, but it wasn't ... the correct version of your father."

Nancy's furrowed brow turned to confusion and frustration

before she broke out in tears. "What does that even mean?" She sobbed. "How am I supposed to keep up with all of this double speak?"

Sebastian was quickly at Nancy's side with a warm hug and a handkerchief. "It will be better soon," he mumbled to her.

I chose to attempt placating her with explanation. "This world is a lot crazier than you thought it was only a few days ago, even with you believing in William's tale. Unfortunately, it is only going to get worse. This world is filled with a lot of things that just don't make sense, and most of them are trying to harm us. The good news is that whatever your father has stumbled into isn't one of those harmful things. I think that he's moved his consciousness into another time." I paused as her sobbing quieted. She was listening, but she wasn't asking any questions. I was so far removed from knowing what a normal reaction was that I just accepted it hoping that I was helping. "I think that he did it to escape the damage of the Blasted Heath. Instead of letting those beasts infect his mind, he simply put his mind somewhere else: another time." Nancy pulled away from Sebastian and used his hanky to wipe her eyes. "When he came back to us he was the wrong William. He was from our future, I think."

"So," Nancy started, "we need to do what exactly? Search time for my father?"

I shook my head. "I don't think so. When your father left his body, he had to leave a piece of himself behind as an anchor, so that he could always come back without getting lost. It is very likely that we have two options available to us for finding your father."

Sebastian asked the next question, genuinely curious. "And those are?"

I frowned. "The easiest method, and the one that I'm against, is to wait. Wherever your father went, I am willing to bet that he's in his own body, in our future. If that's the case, we only need to wait for him to return to us."

"How long will that take?" Nancy asked.

"We have no way of knowing." Sebastian answered.

"What's the second method?"

I looked directly into Nancy's eyes when I answered. She needed to hear it more than Sebastian did. "When I woke your father the first time, I shouted at him that his daughter would die without his help."

"Then shout at him again!" Nancy was getting frustrated.

"It would do no good for me to shout at him." I replied. "He came for you and I think he will do it again."

Nancy was getting frustrated again. Her tears were picking up. She came across the small enclosure and slapped me across the face.

"Give me back my father!"

I understood what was really going on in her head at that moment. I felt so stupid for taking so long to get it. She had lost her father, either in the divorce, the estrangement, or to this madness that now plagued him, and I kept trying to explain to her why her father was gone. I was the only thing providing an explanation for his whereabouts and, instead of calming her down, it was giving her someone to hate. Someone who told her why her father was gone, but hadn't brought him back.

She slapped me twice more before I gathered up her hands and wrapped my arms around her.

"No," I responded. "You're going to do that." I hushed her gently. "Your job from this moment on is to sit beside your father and call out to him. Fill him in on the moments of your life that he missed and let him know that he is safe now and can come home. Home to you." She was still sobbing but she began nodding in the middle of the sobs.

I let her go as she stepped past me and to her father. Nancy slid over a crate with Sebastian's help. Once she was situated comfortably next to her father, Nancy grasped his hand in hers and looked up at me with her still red eyes.

"What should I do? Should I call to him?"

"Just talk to him. Like I said, he missed a big portion of your life. Fill him in on that."

I turned and stepped out of the room, Sebastian following right behind me.

"Andrew," he called after me. "Where are you going?"

"Dawn will be here soon, and with it the ship. I'm going to

go wake Leo so that we can begin moving our supplies to the dock. Right now, at this moment, we are a step ahead of the Germans. I don't want to lose it."

Chapter 7: The Voyage

Once Leo was awake, we set about the task of filling crates and moving them to the dock. The task sounded difficult, but was made all the easier by the twenty men and women that Sebastian sent to help us.

Unlike William's famous Pabodie Expedition, we didn't need nearly as much in the way of supplies as he had. We weren't going to be taking any core samples from the ice or samples of the geology. We also didn't need as many planes. William and the rest of his original crew had needed five planes to take all the scientists further inland. We didn't have anywhere near as many people that needed to go to that terrible city. With only the few of us, it was agreed that one disassembled plane and two dog sleds would be enough.

Of course, I could only acquire one disassembled plane for the Innsmouth warehouse anyway, so it was an easy decision to make.

With all of that decided, we also were not going to be the only people making the trip. Ten of Sebastian's people had decided to accompany us as well, for which I was grateful. The ship was going to need a crew, which would free us up to plan and work on waking up William. Besides, it would leave us with a getaway vehicle if the Nazis decided to give chase.

By the time that the ship had finally pulled into the dock, we had most of the items prepared for loading. I had to force myself not to laugh at Leo's look of disbelief as the ship ramp was lowered.

"Did you dig her up from the bottom of the ocean?" Leo asked.

I managed to replace my urge to laugh with a strong sense of damaged pride. "No, I salvaged her." I led the way up the ship as I explained. "It isn't exactly easy to steal an entire ship from the University, even if it is a University that's more preoccupied with stopping doomsday curses than running a shipyard." As we stepped onto the ship the wood creaked under our feet. "Miskatonic had two former whaling ships that went on the original Pabodie Expedition: the Arkham and the Miskatonic. Those ships were to be sent to scrap a few months ago. I had them rerouted here."

Leo was bouncing lightly behind me on the deck, testing the strength of the wood. "This is only one ship, Andrew, and I'm not sure that it is even that much."

I smiled. "No, this is two ships." I pointed up at the sails and then down at the boards of the deck. If you weren't looking for it, you wouldn't ever see the slight difference in the color of the boards. "Separately, the Arkham and the Miskatonic weren't seaworthy, so I asked the Sebastian and his fellow Innsmouth people to salvage both ships into one new ship."

"Has it been tested?" Leo asked nervously.

I rolled my eyes. "Sebastian takes it out regularly. The Arkatonic has been sea-worthy and tested for the last two months."

"The Arkatonic?" Leo was inspecting the masts with a very concerned eye.

"Yes, the Arkatonic." I paused. "Fine, the name isn't that great, but Sebastian seemed to like it."

Leo stopped investigating the ship and walked over to me, poking me in the chest. "I trust you, but if this ship begins to sink, I'm tying you to the mast." I heard him curse in French as he walked past me and down the ramp. I followed him off the boat and we joined the rest of the Innsmouth people in loading the supplies onto the ship.

The final item to be loaded onto the Arkatonic was William Dyer and his cot. We strapped him to it in order to save him from falling to the deck when the ship rocked. Nancy put a stool next to her father and sat beside him the rest of the morning.

I might have owned the ship, but I knew nothing about it or

sailing. Once the boat was loaded, I set about the very unofficial task of making Sebastian the Captain of the Arkatonic. It was simply a matter of telling him he was, and I was fairly certain that he already expected it. I gave him the route that we were going to take and all the navigational equipment.

The route wasn't something that I had needed to work on too extensively. The original route used by the Pabodie Expedition was still the best viable course for returning to the original camp sites and then the devilish city in the Antarctic. Normally, the current war effort and ramped up U-boat activity by the Germans would also be an added precaution, but the Pabodie route would stay close enough to the continents not occupied by Axis troops to allow us a strong margin of safe passage.

The original Pabodie route would follow south along the eastern North American coast and through the Panama Canal. From there, our next stop will be in Samoa, near Fiji, before we trek to Hobart, Tasmania. Hobart will be our last stop within the civilized world before we trek the last three thousand miles to our first campsite. The entire trip will be between fifteen thousand and sixteen thousand miles and would take us a little over two months to traverse.

The negatives of this method of travel were numerous. For many reasons, we couldn't really tell anyone where we were going. Unlike the original expedition, if we were to go missing, no one would know. Also, our ability to avoid the majority of the war with the U-boats didn't mean that we would be completely in the clear. We had plenty of potential to run afoul of U-boats or Nazi ships. Even though it was unlikely, it could still happen.

Then there was the speed. With an ex-whaler, we could only move as fast as the wind could carry us. Between Sebastian and myself, we could use our magics to keep the wind on our side, but we would still be only a fast moving sailboat. No sailboat could outrun a German ship or submarine crossing the ocean in a race toward alien weaponry. Those ships ran on more powerful things than wind. Our only hope was that we still held the head-start.

Sebastian's ten men boarded and we were ready to leave by noon. The folks that had volunteered had been the most deformed, also known as most human, of the Innsmouth people. All the ostracized Innsmouth folk were actually very decent people, very unlike their cousins. They all would have volunteered, but the more like their cousins they were, even slightly, the more sensitive they were to the sun. More and more creatures of the void, and the spawn birthed of them, were created with an allergy to the radiation provided by modern sunlight. A long time ago, the radiation was something that they could all live with. It was argued that the monsters on the other side of the veil had even craved to live in the light of our stars, but as stars and suns age, their radiations change. Many of the creatures have varying degrees of resistance to the sun based on how long they had managed to live in our world, but still many don't like it.

Innsmouth folk prefer the dark.

That left us with the brave volunteers who still retained the majority of their humanity. The deformed children of Dagon. I went among each of them and thanked them for the sacrifice they were possibly giving. Hopefully, I could bring them all home safely.

The journey began with clear skies. We brought books and games and every form of portable entertainment that we could think of to pass the time, but the best time-waster for me was attempting, yet again, to solve the riddle of William's diary.

I spent hours of each day scribbling into a notebook of my own. I tried taking each of the letters and symbols and assigning them numerical values based on the values I knew them to hold in either the alphabet or the Necronomicon. If I didn't recognize a symbol, I simply assigned it the value of x. I wasted an entire week trying to solve for an equation that didn't exist.

My next effort involved taking the first symbol or letter of what I believed to be the words and reorganizing them all into words and ideas that I recognized. I then tried to form them into a coherent sentence structure, but nothing spoke to me.

That was another week and a half of effort.

I tried every trick and effort to translate, transliterate, or decipher the journal.

Leo spent the time another way. He brushed up on his

English. He worked teaching those that were interested on how to fight and allowed them to teach him how to run the ship. Whenever the words on Dyer's journal started to blur into one horrible mess of ink, I would take a break and it wouldn't be anything special to see Leo helping to turn the sails or tie off some rope that went to some thing. I don't know boats.

Nancy was another story entirely. Her dedication to her father was impressive beyond anything that I would have expected. She fed him and cared for him and she constantly talked to him with absolutely no break except for sleep, which she didn't get much of.

The Panama Canal didn't take as long to traverse as I had assumed, and soon we were back underway and facing the southern waters of the Pacific.

We were five weeks into the voyage when there was finally a breakthrough.

Exasperated, I threw the useless journal against the furthest wall of the small cabin that I shared with Sebastian and Leo. I had just spent three days translating the book backward. I had taken each recognizable configuration of letters, reversed them and attempted a translation. It had been painstaking and mind-numbing. It had also been fruitless.

I stomped off, hoping to find another of Leo's hidden bottles of brandy. Since the voyage had started and Sebastian had shown us our oversight in only stocking one crate of brandy, Leo had quickly moved to hide away as many bottles as he could. It was that or let the poor booze-hound jump overboard and attempt to swim back to Innsmouth.

In my wanderings, I made it back to the very small and cramped compartment where we had shoved William's cot. There was no door, only a cloth covering the opening. When it rained, which it had twice already, we moved William to my slightly larger, and definitely drier, cot and Nancy would share it with him.

I pulled back the curtain to ask Nancy if our rebelling Frenchman had hidden a bottle with her, but as the curtain parted, I saw something I hadn't seen before: William's lips were moving.

It was subtle and his voice was inaudible, but his lips were moving.

Nancy's hands were covering her mouth, leading me to believe that this was an entirely new development.

"What is going on?" I asked quietly, hoping not to surprise Nancy or break whatever had come over William.

Nancy jumped in surprise at my question anyway. William kept moving his lips, completely oblivious to my approach.

"He... I..." Nancy was struggling. "I was ... I was just talking to him, like I have been. His mouth just started moving only a minute ago."

I stepped aside so that Nancy could clear out of my way and I took her seat next to her father. Reaching out, I placed my hand on his forehead and leaned over, placing my ear directly over his mouth.

Still no words came out, but I could almost hear something carrying over his breath. I pushed my will through my hand and into his mind, feeling for his anchor to his body. I found it quickly. It was much stronger than it had been.

"We need to get Sebastian." I said to Nancy.

Sebastian and Leo both came. While this was a little out of Leo's depth, I didn't blame him. Even with every possible form of entertainment aboard the ship, new excitement was always welcome.

Sebastian examined William in much the same manner that I had. He mumbled some sort of spells that I couldn't make out as well, peering into William's eyes as he did so.

Sebastian smiled directly at Nancy when he said, "He's coming back to you."

I could see that Nancy wasn't convinced. "Why isn't he here yet?" She asked.

"He traveled very far," Sebastian answered. "It will take him some more time to finish the journey." We could all see that she wasn't placated by that information. "It won't be long now, girl. Keep talking to him. We might find him back with us before we get to Tasmania."

Even under her disappointment that her father wasn't back yet, Nancy still had a ray of hope that she didn't have before.

We were days away from Samoa and I had given up on the journal completely. Any hope that I was capable of translating the journal I tossed out when Nancy's father began mumbling to himself. I had no doubts that it would be quicker to wait out the geologist. With all of us now anticipating the waking moments of the old man, we began taking turns with him. Nancy wasn't willing to leave her father's side, so we were never alone with him. That was completely fine with all of us. None of us held any sort of delusions about his return. He was coming back for his daughter and she would be the one who brought him back.

Nancy and I made a habit of staying up with her father. She was telling me about how hard it had been reconciling the image of her father that she remembered with the image of her father that the world and her own mother believed in.

"They saw him as a crackpot. A man looking for fame on the backs of his dead colleagues." She explained. Nancy looked at me. "I've seen things since I met you that only prove how right my father was. He had a right to be afraid." I like to think that a normal person would have cried when she said that. Not Nancy. The young lady who I had caught trespassing on my campus was filled with righteous anger. "The world didn't deserve a warning from him."

I couldn't help but agree.

Standing, I left her alone with her father. I was tired and headed back to my bunk.

As I entered, the dark almost completely hid from me that Leo was lying in his own cot. I made it all the way to my own before I noticed his eyes. They were very wide and very open.

"Leo, are you alright?" I asked.

With speed that startled me, Leo sat upright and spun his feet over the edge of his cot. He faced me and stared at me with those wide eyes. My line of work doesn't allow me many moments of fear, but the look in his eyes was alien. I wasn't looking at Leo.

His mouth started working and small noises began coming out. They were odd noises. First he was wheezing and then half words were coming out.

Finally he said, "This takes some getting used to."

While the voice was his, the words were definitely not.

He tilted his head to the side and worked his mouth a little more before the next words came out.

"Time … is different for me … here," he said. Not-Leo paused again. "Do you … remember … the long-lived child?"

It took me much longer than it should have to figure out what he was talking about. It was so out of context. Once the voyage had gotten underway and we had some time to sit and rest, I had explained fully about that situation. He had no reason to be mentioning it, though. When it finally came to me, I was just as surprised as I was confused.

He was referencing the ancient child. The boy at the border of the Dream Lands. Why would he be mentioning that?

"Yes," was all that I said to him. I was beginning to piece together what was going on. The more that I figured out, the more furious I became.

"After … after I escaped…" he trailed off and the look in his eyes became distant for a moment before he snapped back to me. "It took me weeks to remember the spell that you taught him." He took a deep breath. "It took me weeks to learn how to summon the Gaunt."

"No," I gasped with the confirmation.

"It is different controlling a body without the help of those inside it." He laughed and it sounded so foreign, as if they had just learned how to do it. "I have been lying in that bed for … well … time has a different meaning for me here … but I've been lying there for a while trying to figure out how this," he waved indicating himself, "all works."

"Olivia…" I said.

"You don't get to talk," she interrupted. "You sold me when all I wanted to do was help you." Her anger sounded so violent, and I couldn't figure out if it was because her voice was being filtered through Leo's or if she was so violently close to lunging at me.

"You will be ejected the minute that Leo wakes up."

She laughed her foreign laugh again. It grated on my ears. "Not if I kill him first."

"Don't you—"

Olivia interrupted me again. "Don't I what? Betray you? Kill your friend? No! You have no right to tell me what to do." She was spitting as she shouted. "I will control your allies in their sleep. You will forever be haunted by me." Olivia started to cry. "We were allies…"

"No!" I was shouting back at her. "You were a disease that plagued my mind. I never wanted you in my life and when I had a chance to get rid of you I took it!"

She was whimpering. "You do not know what Timmy did to me." She sobbed again. "You don't know what he does to all of the creatures that he collects."

Guilt washed over me, but I didn't want it there. She was humanizing herself again, but she wasn't a human. She was a broken piece of myself. "I am sorry for whatever happened to you. I was wrong for how I got rid of you, but that doesn't give you the right to control anyone." I shrugged and waved my hands at Leo's body. "What is the purpose of this?"

Olivia ignored the tears on her face, but suddenly her sobbing was done. "I am not certain, yet, but I know that I want to hurt you." She leaned toward me. "It isn't fair that you get to live in this world while I live as a fugitive in another. So, I want you to suffer and I want to live here."

I slapped Leo across the face, hoping that it would wake him up. It didn't work. "What's the point of taking them over? Take my mind, as I sleep. Control me and drive me mad all over again, but leave them alone."

She frowned and it was the first thing she did that looked natural. "I attempted to, but the emptiness in your mind that was once me stops me from controlling you."

I growled in frustration. Words were failing me.

"Sleep with one eye open, Andrew. I love this world and if I can't live here as I once did, then I will live here however I can." Olivia pulled a knife from somewhere hidden in the dark. The small amount of light in the room glinted off the blade. For a fast moment, I thought that she was going to lunge at me. "I will make you suffer!" She said again and then brought the blade down into Leo's left leg.

Olivia laughed, as if the pain wasn't touching her at all, and the alien laughter morphed into a gasping pain that no longer sounded like her. Instead, it carried a French accent.

The screams had been out of surprise and not so much pain. Leo looked down at his hand still grasping the knife and the shouting turned toward gasps.

He looked at me and asked, "Was it Olivia?"

Leo's intuition surprised me. "How did you know?"

He began tearing his pant leg open and examining the wound. "Two nights ago, I woke up and I was standing at the front of the boat." He waved at our door. "Last night, Nancy was standing right there and watching both of us. It was very odd." It was comforting knowing for certain that this was Leo. His movements and his voice were all his own. Not the possessing demon that I gave birth to.

"How did you know it was Olivia?" I asked.

Leo began tearing one of his sheets into strips. "I guessed. After hearing how you left her in the Dream Lands, I was kind of worried that she might come back." He pulled the knife from his leg and began wrapping it with the strips as quickly as he could.

He asked, "Why was she here?"

"Payback," I replied. "She wants to hurt me by hurting my allies."

"Lock me up when I sleep," Leo suggested.

I shook my head. "Then Nancy is holding a gun to my head and you're nowhere to be found."

"Lock us all up."

"That won't work either." I sighed and lit the lantern between our cots. "Then you're shooting yourself in your sleep, or Nancy is bashing her head against a wall. We can't fight this by tying our hands."

Leo finished bandaging his leg and looked at me. "Then we are powerless to stop her."

I shook my head again. "No. We can beat her, I just need to think on it."

"Think quickly," my friend smiled, but the smile didn't make it to his eyes. "I would hate to wake up with my hands around your neck."

I nodded and laid down to sleep. I was somehow comforted knowing that the lantern was still on.

I wasn't asleep an hour when another voice jerked me awake. I sat bolt upright and it took me a moment to recognize the voice.

Leo was already on his feet and said, "It's Nancy." Together we made our way quickly to her. We would have run to her, but Leo's wound was obviously causing him pain.

Nancy was standing outside the small half-room that her father's cot was in.

"He's awake!"

"Get back!" I was shouting just as loudly as she was, but my words confused her. Leo grabbed her by the shoulders and gently directed her to the side. I drew my pistol and stepped into the room.

William Dyer was sitting up on his cot, his hands rubbing his face.

I put the barrel of my gun against his forehead.

"Dr. Dyer, I presume?"

He looked up at me slowly, wary of the gun. "What is the meaning of …wait a minute. I know you, don't I?" He looked at me, wrinkling his eyes as he did so. "Yes, you're that silly boy who wanted to see the book get locked away." He let out a laugh. "Andy, wasn't it? You gave the Dean quite the heartache." He was smiling despite the gun. "Well, I think that you should know that I fought for your way of thinking." He pointed at the gun in my hands. "You can either use that or don't. I don't have all day."

I was furrowed my brow. If it was her, then it was a great deception. "Nancy, get in here," I called.

Nancy came in with Leo right behind. I put the pistol away before she could see it. "Ask him something only your father would know. Do it now."

She was confused, but managed to ask, "What did you get me for my last birthday that we shared?"

William frowned and shook his head. "That was years ago, darling."

I drew the pistol and put it to his head again. Nancy started shouting "No," over and over again while Leo quickly moved to hold her in place.

"Answer the questions, please, Dr. Dyer." I said while pulling back the hammer on the pistol. I didn't want to shoot him, and Leo knew that, but Nancy had no idea. Rage filled her eyes and she fought even harder against Leo's grip.

On the other hand, if Olivia was currently wearing William's body, the magically charged bullet had a very good chance of actually killing her and finally removing her from the situation.

William remained unperturbed throughout the entire situation.

He sighed and looked directly at his daughter. "I gave you money and begged you to keep an eye on your mother for me."

I looked away from William and to his daughter for confirmation. She nodded emphatically. "It's him!" She shouted.

The shouting was unnecessary. We had already gathered a few of the Innsmouth people behind us. They were watching with the kind of excitement that only a little over a month at sea could produce.

I uncocked the pistol and put it back into my holster. "Welcome back, Dr. Dyer."

"Do you mind my asking what that was about?" William asked while his daughter pushed past me to hug him profusely.

The actual reason for my holding a gun on Nancy's father was something that I didn't want to share with anyone that I didn't have to. I looked to Leo with a look begging him to save me from the truth, but he had nothing, so I grabbed the first thing that I could think of.

"You've been an empty husk for over a month. People who have seen the … things that we have can't take it for granted when a body just gets up without any warning."

William was no idiot, and he recognized that what I was saying couldn't be the whole truth, but he refrained from saying so. Instead, the geologist gave me a small nod.

As Nancy released her father, William scratched the silver beard that covered his chin and asked, "Where are we?"

I wasn't certain how he was going to react when I told him, so I opted for taking the long path.

"The German army has discovered something that could end the war in their favor, we're in a race to get it."

He looked around, eyeing the walls of the small cabin he occupied. He slapped his foot down on the boards.

William returned his eyes to me. They were wide and darted about in his skull. "We're on a boat?"

I nodded. "We need your help, Dr. Dyer."

He laughed nervously. "I bet you do." He tried to stand, but his legs were too weak and he fell back onto the cot. "There are only two places that a rebellious student from Miskatonic could possibly want to take 'Old-Man-Dyer,' and I doubt that you're preparing for spelunking in Australia!"

William's nervous laughter had turned into manic shouting.

"Father," Nancy said, "they are going to go into that city you described and they are going to take everything they can." She grabbed William by the chin and pulled his terror filled eyes away from me and forced him to look her in the eye. "Those things you saw, do you want them in the real world? Because that's what is going to happen if you don't help us."

William's eyes kept searching about as if looking for the real world again. Finally, they fell on Nancy and his look began to calm. He reached up and touched his daughter's face gently. After staring at her for a moment longer he turned his attention back to me.

"What can I do to help?"

Leo handed me the journal and I passed it to William. "Tell us what this says."

He looked it over as if it were some foreign object from some long dead civilization. The geologist took his time scanning it before finally cracking it open. William flipped through the pages, squinting as he did so. He paused on several different places within the book before continuing to the next section.

"Interesting…" he mumbled. "Where did you find this?"

"In your cabin in Utah," I answered.

He furrowed his brow, "My cabin?" He looked confused. "I haven't been there since…" Suddenly his eyes went wide. "Oh my…"

I had waited so long to know what was going on in that

damned book that my frustration was only growing. "What is 'oh my'?"

"This is the journal I wrote while on the Pabodie Expedition. I used it to explain the difficulties we came across in the city." He frowned. "I thought I was writing it in English, but that city plays with your mind. I can read most of it, but some of it will have to wait until we're back in the city." William shrugged. "These are instructions for safely navigating the city. It is a map, more or less."

I smiled. I was genuinely happy. We would be able to use the journal in the city and the Germans were left without help. Even if they managed to get ahead of us, the city had the potential to destroy them, whereas the journal would help us stay safe.

"What about the words in the margin?" Nancy asked.

William squinted his eyes as he looked at what his daughter was referencing. "'It will devour the world'?" He looked to Nancy and then myself. "I must have written it in the city. I don't know what it references."

While I was elated by knowing how we could properly use the book, I was slightly disturbed by the reference in the margin that not even William knew why he had written it.

Pointing at William and then Nancy, I said, "You both have a new and old assignment. Study the book. Tell us everything that you can before we get there. Using it in the city will be helpful, but knowing what we're going into will be more useful."

I stuck my hand out to William, this time without a pistol in it. He took it slowly, and we shook. "Welcome aboard, Dr. Dyer. Tonight, catch up with your daughter. Tomorrow morning, I would like to pick your brain on what you've been through. Everything." The geologist noticeably blanched when I said the last word.

He had seen the worst that the other worlds had to offer our own and it was too much to hope that he would be as interested in tackling that world again as I was. William Dyer was a victim that I intended to use. I hoped that he was up for it.

The next day, I pumped every bit of information about the city out of William that I could. Unfortunately, he had been very thorough in his manuscript to the press. Doubly unfortunate was his time away from the city. In an effort to rebuild his broken reputation that had only been saved by tenure within the university, he had taken on other jobs and expeditions across the globe, including the one that he previously mentioned to me that had taken place in Australia. Whatever happened there, though, had not been important enough to share with me. Yet, anyway.

On that note, I asked Nancy and Leo to refrain from sharing with William the fact that a future version of himself had pushed through to our timeline. I doubted that telling him would cause any undue stress, but not telling him definitely wasn't causing any undue stress. The decision was easy, and if the need arose for him to know about his exploits in the world of H. G. Wells, then I would share that information immediately.

We left Samoa a few days after William returned to us. During that time, aside from interviewing him about what he knew, I left him to translate the journal with his daughter. While I truly thought the work would mean the difference between the failure and success of this mission, I also was hoping that he would get some much needed time to relearn his daughter.

I spent the time with Leo. Without the journal to fill my time, I joined him in his studies on the ship. Samoa gave us time to restock some of our supplies before the last big resupply in Hobart, Tasmania. It also gave Leo and I a chance to take stock of our weapon situation. I purchased more bullets and went with Leo to find more guns. He was well armed, but having an extra rifle or two couldn't hurt.

The evenings after William was awake were fun, to say the least. Leo brought out some of his hidden bottles and we sat with the crew drinking and laughing and getting to know each other better. This was when we learned the truth about the Australian expedition.

William had been brought along as a colleague of his, a Nathaniel Wingate Peaslee. As it would turn out, Peaslee had been pulled forcefully from his body to live among an alien species for five years. The expedition revealed even more. It was a species that had lived on Earth for a period of time and as they died out, they preferred to live on in the bodies of other beings, allowing them to die in their place. Peaslee had been sent to the past without his consent.

Time travel.

The mirrors to what had happened to William were not lost on me, and I did my best to find out how exactly he had learned the secret of moving his mind.

"How," I asked as I passed the bottle of brandy to Nancy, "did you escape the torture of the Blasted Heath?"

He nodded, eyeing his daughter as she swigged from the bottle. "Dean Smythe was begging me to meet with some of his colleagues. He wanted me to tell them everything that I could recall about those damned mountains..." He began to drift, keeping his eyes on the bottle as it passed from hand to hand. "Smythe said that we would be saving the world. It wasn't that I didn't trust him, it was that I did not want to revisit that horrible place. Not even in the words of an interview." William shook his head, trying to bring himself back to the here and now. "I know Arkham and that dreaded book, so it wasn't hard for me to figure out that the Blasted Heath would keep me hidden well. Unfortunately, I didn't know that the same forces that keep people out, would stop me from leaving."

The bottle made its way back to William and he took a deep pull before passing it to Leo. "Peaslee taught me a neat trick when we were voyaging back to the campus. He taught me how to leave my body behind and traverse the waves of space ... and time." He shuddered again. "I figured that if my mind was not in my body, then the Blasted Heath couldn't steal it from me. So, I left."

It all was exactly as I had suspected. This led me to believe that, with William knowing that during a specific period of time his body would not be occupied by his consciousness, he was able to reach back to that time and easily re-inhabit his body. Time travel within his own form.

Hobart was our last stop before we would be making shore on the Antarctic continent. We were very specific in checking the numbers on all our supplies. Once the boat was completely stocked and any sort of issues had been dealt with, Sebastian and I agreed that everyone could have a night to themselves on land. Even with the strong seafaring history of the Sebastian's people of Innsmouth, they were generations removed from actual sea travel.

All our homes were on land, and we missed it. The night was necessary.

The next morning, we went back to the seas. We had begun dressing warmer as we came into Hobart, and dressed even warmer once we left.

At eight weeks of travel, we finally started seeing land. Vast and lofty, snow-clad mountains stretched across the horizon and I immediately began to recall the beautiful descriptions that William had used in his reference to the press. More and more we saw him on the deck, staring out over that mountain chain. His face was blank, but his eyes spoke of the dread that he saw there.

I walked to him one of those times and he began to mumble to me. I stepped closer to hear him over the wind and found him saying, "The Admiralty Range, originally discovered by Ross. So dreadfully beautiful..." I left him to it, but told Nancy that she should collect her father and bring him in for the night before he froze. She knew I meant more than that. She knew that I worried that her father may not have fully returned to us. His sanity had been tested more than any one man's ever should.

We enjoyed the sites the next several days as we rounded Cape Adare and sailed down the east coast of Victoria Island. William continued to narrate the journey to us, but I had read his words enough times that he didn't need to narrate at all. I could have described it all for him with my eyes closed.

Following the coast we came upon the shore of McMurdo Sound, at the base of the volcano Erebus. The wind was tearing out our sails and our bodies. We were so cold that we began lighting fires at every chance that we could.

Unlike in Dyer's words, Erebus wasn't smoking, but behind it I could still make out the extinct volcano Mount Terror.

The shore of McMurdo was exactly where we needed to be and I could tell that William wasn't happy with it at all. He had stopped talking altogether in the last day. At least that was the case with us. I asked Nancy about it and she said that he was speaking when he had something important to say but he was hurting.

"He lost many friends and colleagues here. He isn't only visiting a terrifying city among the mountains, he is also visiting the graves of men that he was forced to leave behind."

I understood the guilt that he felt. I had felt it whenever someone I knew or traveled with had passed on. It made little sense to me how I had managed to survive so long while so many who had chosen to fight my war had died. I was regularly surprised that Leo was still alive and willing to fight the good fight.

By the time that we began launching the small boats toward the shore, we had been traveling for nine weeks and five days. It had been a long trip and while we were dreading the cold journey ahead, we were excited to be loading into the boats. We rowed to shore and brought cables with each boat. Each cable led back to the ship to breeches-buoy supplies from the boat to the shore.

A breeches-buoy is a means of using cables and pulleys to shuttle supplies over the water and to the shore. It's a very convenient means of moving some of our heavier equipment without having to load it into each boat and row back and forth between the ship and the shore. It also minimized the chances that we would be losing any of the supplies into the water. They had used a similar system on the first voyage, and I had made certain that the Arkatonic was outfitted with the same equipment. The dogs hated it, so we took them over in the boats.

Sebastian and his crew stayed aboard the Arkatonic. We wouldn't need them from this point out unless it would be as support from the boat or during some necessarily quick getaway. Besides, I could tell that most of the crew would rather stay on the much warmer boat. Once the supplies had been moved to the shore, they took all the boats and returned to the ship.

On the shore of McMurdo Sound stood myself, Leo, Nancy, and William. That was my entire entourage, and I was happier for it.

We began by setting up our tents. I left that tent-work to

Nancy and William while Leo and I set about piecing together the small aircraft.

A crack, like thunder, made us drop everything. Leo and I spun, pistols drawn, while Nancy and her father dropped to their knees, hands over their heads.

More than thirty Germans, in Nazi winter gear and with their own sleds and dogs, surrounded our soon-to-be camp. How they had managed to sneak up on us, I had no idea. There were so many of them that I had no idea where to aim my pistol. For good measure, I drew my sword as well.

Leo had only the one pistol up and aimed; his other armaments were in a crate by the tents.

From somewhere in the middle of the pack of Nazis came a smaller and much older man. Without fear he walked all the way to me and Leo. We kept our guns on him, but I recognized him, and the confusion brought on by my recognition halted any sort of attack that I might have mounted.

Similarly, Leo was halted by his common sense. You never shoot at a man with an army directly behind him. It's an easy way to get yourself killed.

"Captain James Sterling?" I asked. "From the train in Utah."

Without a German accent, and a hint of southern charm, the much older gentleman nodded and said, "My real name is Befehlsleiter Erich Strobel."

Befehlsleiter was the high ranking title of Command Leader. It was impressive.

Strobel stood straighter than he had on the train. Straighter and stronger. Captain James Sterling had been an act.

His next words were in his native born accent. "I have been using the identity of the good Captain to keep tabs on you. It allowed me to properly position my men as well. Captain Sterling was able to recruit your American-styled cultists and zealots." He smiled and it seemed a genuinely nice smile. "We had to keep an eye on you, and I preferred not to trust such important details to lesser staff."

I tightened my grip on my weapons. "What happens now?" I felt bile rising in my throat. No matter how pleasant this aggressor was, he was still the enemy. He had stalked me and played me at every turn and now that I was finally a step ahead, he was showing me that I was actually two steps behind.

"Now, you lower your weapons. Then I will take your companions with me. We will infiltrate the city, take what we came for, and leave."

I smirked. "You failed to mention what part I would play in all of that."

"Dr. Doran, you have more than earned my respect through your past exploits. I would not do you the disservice of bringing you along with your companions. You will die here and not plague me in the future."

He saw my grip tighten and a contingent of no less than ten soldiers stepped forward and aimed their weapons at the Dyer family.

"There is no need for this to play out. I have no intention of killing your companions once we are done with them. I shall return them to this spot, giving them a chance to survive."

Strobel directed several of his men to collect Leo's weapons, which they did, and to tie up the hands of Leo, Nancy, and William. They left me untouched and standing completely still as they worked around me.

I was not surprised that they had left me with my weapons. Guns have no value to a dead man.

Once my companions were well-secured, Strobel said in German, "Send the message. Tell them to destroy the ship."

One of his men withdrew a radio set and began cranking it.

Shouting, "No!" I drew my pistol and fired twice into the radio.

More than thirty guns were drawn on me. Before they could shoot, I dropped my gun onto my boot so that it wouldn't sink into the snow. I threw my hands over my head.

Strobel walked over to me, anger flashed across his face. "You have only cost us a radio. If our ship does not hear from us within the hour, they will destroy the ship anyway."

I smirked, "Then I have bought myself some time."

Erich Strobel strode a few feet away from me. "I told you, Dr. Doran, my respect for you means that I will not be giving you so many chances as you have received in the past."

He spun in the snow and smoothly drew a pistol.

The explosion from the gun didn't register nearly as loudly to me as the punch to my chest as the bullet hit me.

I sunk enough into the snow to see the bright red getting absorbed by it. I could hear them screaming. Leo and Nancy were hollering. I looked to the right and could only see William. Terror was across his face, and instead of screaming, he was struggling against his bonds.

Fight, old man. I thought. *Fight every chance that you can.*

The cold was replaced by the dark.

Chapter 8: The Ice

While the blackness that consumed me had done so quickly, returning to the waking world seemed to take much longer. My chest hurt near my heart and the pain radiated out and toward my shoulder. It was a dull ache that made my entire upper torso stiff.

I opened my eyes slowly, allowing them to adjust for the light. I was in a wooden room, boards lining the ceiling. I attempted to sit up, but the pain turned from dull to sharp as I did so and threatened to engulf me in darkness again.

A hand touched my right shoulder and lowered me back down to wherever I was lying. I turned my head slowly and saw Sebastian looking down at me.

"Andrew, you have been shot. I need you to relax and tell me what happened." He asked.

"Where am I?" I asked, suddenly very concerned.

Sebastian frowned in confusion, but answered. "We heard a gunshot and assumed something had gone wrong. I sent a man through the breeches-buoy to check on you. Everyone was gone and you had been shot near your shoulder, so I had you brought back to the Arkatonic."

I started shaking my head and tried to get up, but Sebastian pushed me back onto the cot again. "We need to leave now!" I shouted. The effort of yelling sent another wave of pain through my body, but I ignored it and continued to struggle against him.

"Why?" He returned.

"How long?" I demanded. "How long has it been since you heard the gunshot?"

Sebastian shook his head, surrendering and allowing me to

sit up. "About an hour. Andrew, why does it matter?"

I jumped to my feet and did my best to ignore the dizziness that attempted to claim me. "Germans were waiting for us. Nazis, a lot of Nazis." I found where Sebastian had put my weapons and winter clothing. I began putting them on. "They were going to sink the boat. I shot their radio before they could call in the order, but if their ship doesn't receive communication from them in an hour they have orders to sink the Arkatonic anyway!"

Sebastian was at a loss for words and could only mumble, "What?"

I grabbed him by the shoulders and shook him, wincing as the pain shot up my left arm. I growled through the pain. "Get to the boats!"

The boat rocked with an explosion. No alarm had gone up before the explosion, which led me to believe that the Germans were traveling by submarine.

The explosion rocked the boat wildly enough to send me and Sebastian sprawling to the deck. I used my good arm to help Sebastian to his feet as I got to my own. Together we ran for the edge of the boat. The explosion had thrown some of the crew from the ship while others were scrambling to man their stations. Sebastian had to yell at them to get to the boats to snap them out of their own confusion.

The Arkatonic listed heavily forward as it began to sink. The sudden tipping of the ship lifted many of us into the air before gravity caught us and brought us back down. We all slid across the deck, even more of the Innsmouth folk went over and into the icy waters.

Another explosion tipped the ship even further, and the housing for the small row boats couldn't take the strain. The housing snapped and the boats fell into the water.

"Damn!" I shouted. Sebastian mouthed the words as we both grabbed onto the nearest mast to stay above the water. My chest was screaming in pain as the deck pitched. My grip threatened to break.

"If we hit the water then we might as well say goodbye to your companions." Sebastian shouted.

He was right of course. The freezing waters might not kill us, but if we made it to the shore and the campsite it would take too long to dry ourselves and our clothes. By the time that we would finally catch up with Strobel and his ilk, we would have lost too much time. We had already lost an hour to my damned bullet wound, we couldn't afford to lose too much more. The more time that the Nazis were in the city, the more likely that our planet was doomed.

Holding onto that mast, an idea struck me hard enough to almost dislodge me. A thick rope whipped back from the edge of the Arkatonic and struck my leg, I grunted and looked at where it had come from.

The breeches-buoy.

"Sebastian!" I shouted. "The buoy!"

He caught on immediately. "How will we get there?"

The question was valid, the ship was already at least standing at 45 degrees. I reached out to the void, touching that dreadful magic that had become my calling. Using my will-power and the rules of physics that came from beyond the veil, I anchored both of our feet to the deck. I let go of the mast and looked to Sebastian.

"I can't hold it for long. Let's move."

The strain from the void was only slightly worse than the strain of gravity had been when I was holding the mast. I would be slipping soon.

We ran across the deck as men slid past us and came to the breeches-buoy.

The basket was larger than was usual, refitted to deal with the larger crates we had needed to move to the shore. Somehow in the chaos the pulley had been damaged and the basket had fallen into the icy waters.

I pulled my sword and cut a length of thick anchor rope, and then another. "We'll loop it over the top and slide down," I explained.

Sebastian nodded before amending, "You will." I was confused until he nodded toward the point where the breeches-buoy anchored to the side of the boat.

The bolts were already warped and they were getting worse as we watched.

"Damn!" I shouted and almost threw the lengths of rope that I had collected.

Sebastian placed his hand on my shoulder. "I can support it," he grabbed the length of rope that he was supposed to use to slide to the shore. "I should be able to hold it long enough for you to get across."

I shook my head. "You will die. I can't let you do that, not for me."

He barked a laugh. "Then for who shall I die? No one has done as much for me and my people as you have. We owe you so much." Sebastian wrapped his rope around the smaller mast that anchored the breeches-buoy assembly to the side of the ship. He pulled, bracing himself against the side of the ship as strain entered his face. "I don't plan on dying. I'm strong Innsmouth stock and I can handle the icy currents. Start a fire for me in the camp and I will be there nice and warm when you return."

I couldn't argue with his determination. I needed to be the one to get to the shore if I was going to stop Strobel. Sebastian was good people, though, and he shouldn't have to die. On the other hand, he was also right about his genetics. If anyone could survive this ship sinking into those dark icy waters, it would be Sebastian and his crew.

I hoped so anyway.

I nodded to him and clasped his shoulder. "Thank you, friend. I expect to see you on that shore." Sebastian smiled through his straining face and nodded back.

"Go!"

I threw the rope over the buoy cable and leapt.

The ship shuddered and shook through the rope as I slid down the cable and toward the shore. The lurching of the cable in reply to the sinking ship threatened to buck me off on multiple occasions, but I made it to the shore, only barely. As soon as the ice and snow were under me, the rope, and supposedly Sebastian, let go. I fell the remaining six feet and rolled into the snow.

I got to my feet as quickly as I could and turned to look at the ship. It had sunk almost half into the water and it was speeding up. I couldn't see Sebastian anywhere, but I had also let go of the magic holding him to the deck once he grabbed onto the breeches-buoy. Hopefully, he had gotten away from the undertow.

Turning away from the sight of the ship and whatever subsequent explosions planned to follow, I made my way back to the camp. The breeches-buoy was supposed to get the crates to the shore, but the shore was too windy for the campsite. With that in mind, the campsite was moved about a hundred yards more inland. It didn't help much, as the entire continent was covered with a really strong wind, but it made a small difference.

The first thing that I did was round up the three dogs. I wasn't going to be walking through the snow to catch up to Strobel and his men. I tied the dogs all to the sled and threw them some meat from one of the crates.

Then I grabbed the weapon crate, a snow suit, snowshoes, bedding, and a tent and strapped them down on the sled. While the dogs finished the meat, I moved each of the crates and the other tents much closer together. I piled the crates into a makeshift wall to block the wind and began putting together a fire with our extra firewood.

I covered the wood with some of the extra fuel we brought along for the plane. Within minutes I had a raging fire sitting about six feet away from a large stack of supplies and a tent. Hopefully, Sebastian and whatever men he found would be able to find it before they froze to death.

The secondary hope that I had for the fire was that Strobel and his men would see the smoke and figure it was whatever was left of the boat. Maybe Sebastian and his crew would be able to last long enough for me to successfully complete my mission, find some means of sailing back to America, and actually return back to them with said means.

Yes, it was impossible, but I was moving forward by taking it one piece at a time.

The first piece was to follow Strobel and his Nazi army into the heart of the terrible alien city.

I yelled "Mush," and allowed the dogs to pull me in the direction of the army's tracks.

Before the dogs and I had taken off, I had also slipped more of the winter attire from the crates. I was grateful that I had. The wind tore at my face and clothes as the dogs carried me over the snow.

I kept glancing over my shoulder, long after the shore was out of sight, to see any sign of Sebastian and his clan of Innsmouth folk. Of course, there was no sign.

Pulling the coat hood tighter around my face, I yelled again for the dogs.

Even though they had an hour head start, I hadn't expected Strobel to be traveling as quickly as he was. The miscalculation on my part was that I assumed they were traveling on foot. The winds had picked up considerably since the sinking of the Arkatonic, but the drifting snows hadn't covered all their tracks. About three miles from the shore I found paths of kicked up snow that led toward the mountains. Each path was approximately twelve feet wide.

The Germans were in vehicles. My guess was that they rode in large trucks on treads. I wasn't going to be catching up with them at all. Quite the opposite, actually. The Germans were going to pull away from me.

I kept the dogs moving and tried to calculate how I would catch up with my quarry.

The short answer was that I couldn't. The trucks could travel at probably twice the speed of the dogs and still retain a semblance of a safe speed. They also wouldn't need to rest, which the beautiful dogs leading my sled most definitely would. The trucks were also protecting their men from the harsh winds. I wasn't protected at all and the wind wasn't only chilling me, but it was also draining me of energy. I would need to rest just as much as the dogs would.

That night, I did just that. I couldn't keep the dogs running as hard as I wanted and the wind was beginning to get colder and harsher as the evening hours came. I stopped the sled and we rested. It was three hours before I opened my eyes again. The tent from the crates kept most of the cold wind off me, and I was using a small kerosene heater to keep the cold from killing me. I had also pulled the dogs into the tent with me. Four dogs, a kerosene heater, and stubborn Dean was enough to keep me from losing any toes.

The plan had been to travel straight through the night, but I hadn't been prepared for how cold the nights in the Antarctic were. In hindsight, that sounds kind of dumb, but when you've faced down as many monsters and climates as I had, you just started expecting to be prepared.

The cold kept me from sleeping the rest of the night and as soon as the dogs began to stir, I packed up the camp and hooked the dogs back to the sled. I pulled my wrappings and coat tight around me and took off after the Germans again.

My first break came about an hour after I took off. The sun was glistening off the snow with such blinding light that I kept my eyes closed most of the time, only opening them to make sure that we were still following the path the Germans had carved into the snow. I had lucked out in that regard. The winds from the previous night hadn't destroyed the trail the Germans had been making.

It was during one of those stretches with my eyes closed that I heard it. It started so quietly and sounded like a buzz, as if a swarm of bees were approaching my location. It grew steadily louder and I began casting my eyes around looking for the sound.

My eyes saw it, but the idea was so strange that it took me a moment to realize what I was looking at.

A small plane was flying low and along the trail that I had been etching across the fields of ice and snow. It came in low, roaring louder as it approached. Instead of wheels, the landing gear consisted of skis. It was a clever design that would work well to land on the unsure ground, and one I had seen only once before.

The plane was the same plane that had been left disassembled in its respective crates at the campsite near shore. It was the plane that I had originally planned on using for getting to the terrible city.

And it was coming lower, intending a landing just behind me. I didn't know what to think. Either Sebastian and his men had survived, or the Nazis from the submarine come ashore and decided to use the supplies they found to chase down their companions.

The plane bounced twice on the ice about a mile behind me. The skis kept it from sinking into the white, but the plane would require a long runway to make up its lack of brakes. The dogs immediately laid down, and I grew concerned that if the plane was aimed at me I wouldn't be able to get them moved out of the way in time.

As the plane grew closer, I realized the dogs and my sled were safe. The plane came up on my left and it slid by faster than I could get a look at who was inside, but slow enough to come to a stop only a few hundred yards in front of me. I hollered at the dogs and shook the reins to get them standing. They resisted because of how tired they already were but were up within moments.

I gripped my pistol, pulling it from my coat as the dogs raced toward the landed aircraft.

Pulling on the reins, I slowed the dogs down and jumped off the sled, letting the dogs and it come to a rest on their own. I ran as quickly as my winter-wear would let me directly for the co-pilot door. The door flew open in my grip and I shoved my pistol in, taking aim at the pilot.

Sebastian grinned at me with his hands in the air. "Need a lift?"

He was the only person in the plane, so I put the gun away. "How the hell did you get here?" I asked.

Sebastian lowered his hands. "Between your warning and the blazing fire you left on the shore, most of us survived the attack on the Arkatonic," he frowned. "We began taking stock and as soon as I found the plane, I knew what I had to do." He waved at the sled and dogs out in front of the plane. "They won't get you there with enough time to be any good." Sebastian slapped his hands down on the plane. "This will."

Elation swept through me. I had been in such a rush to go after the Germans that I hadn't even thought about taking the time to piece the plane together. In all fairness, I probably couldn't have done it by myself, and I was grateful for the Innsmouth folk that had managed to piece it together.

I frowned. "What about the dogs?"

"We can bring them with us or leave them behind." Sebastian didn't look very happy. "Either way, Andrew, they'll probably freeze to death."

He was right. Even if took the dogs with us, they would freeze in the plane once we left them to take on the city. Logically, I should leave them to fend for themselves as long as they could, but those dogs had been nothing but faithful during my day and a half trip. I owed them better.

Once the dogs were loaded into and around the back two seats of our little four-person plane, I climbed into the copilot seat. Sebastian was petting some of the dogs. Once I was in and secure he turned to me.

"We don't need to catch the Nazis, just get to the city." He pointed out the window. "Is it that way?" Sebastian was pointing the way that I had been heading.

I pulled out the papers regarding the original Dyer expedition and scanned them. "Yes. That mountain in the distance is one of the outer walls to Dyer's city. The whole range hides the city ... protects it. Once we get over those mountains," I mimed Sebastian's pointing out the window. "Let's get this over with."

The plane roared to life, and within minutes the dogs and I were leaving the sled far behind as we approached what I hoped would be the final leg of our journey.

Chapter 9: The Mountains

II We'll do a flyby," Sebastian was shouting over the roar of the wind and the tiny plane's engine. "I'll take the plane around the city to find a place to … land."

Sebastian sounded unsure of the word "land," and I didn't blame him. No modern day cities had airfields, why would an ancient alien city be any different in that regard? That being said, it sounded as if there was something else hidden behind his struggling with the word.

"What's wrong?" I asked him.

Sebastian's smile was weak as he explained. "Andrew, I might be considered the failed half-breed of the family, but my people only know the sea." He shrugged, tightening his grip on the yoke as the turbulence bounced the plane. "Flying has been surprisingly easy, but I have never flown or landed before today."

I had suspected as much with how tightly he had been gripping the yoke for the entire flight.

"Have you," Sebastian asked me slowly, "ever landed a plane before?"

I laughed, figuring I was damned anyway, I might as well laugh at the universe. "No." I forced a straight look onto my face and ignored the husky trying to lick my face. "I have all the faith in the world in your ability to bring this plane down."

Sebastian caught my words and returned my smile. "As do I," he laughed.

"So," I asked, "what was your incentive to use the plane?"

Sebastian shrugged in the tight cockpit. "It was either save you with the plane or let you freeze to death."

I nodded, "A crash is quicker, I'll give you that."

The mountains rose in front of us, filling most of the view. They were unlike other mountains that I had been to in that they were taller, sharper, and completely covered in white, instead of just capped. Some of them had black-as-night sides leading to the white-capped mountains.

Maybe it was the reasoning behind us being there, or maybe it was just my imagination, but those black scrapings on the sides of those mountains looked as if they had been created by beings much larger than our little plane.

My nerves were already worn, so it didn't really affect me aside from the casual observation. I filed it away in the back of my mind, hoping that I wouldn't have to fight something large enough to peel snow from the sides of mountains.

Within minutes the mountains were taking up the entire view in front of us. As we crested the short valley between two of the peaks, Sebastian tilted the plane and put the city that we were looking for directly in my field of view.

The mountains formed a perfect bowl shape, as if something had crashed into the Earth, creating a crater that froze into the shape of the mountains. In the center of the crater rested what I could only describe as the city that we were looking for. The sun seemed to be non-existent in the basin of the crater, but enough residual light touched the inside walls of the bowl to make out the city.

It existed on multiple planes of reality. Which is a lazy way of explaining what it was that I was looking at. The dark city was protruding from angles that didn't exist in our reality. What I was looking at wasn't entirely new to me. I had seen similar structures any time that I had crossed into the reality next to ours.

Any time that I had crossed into the veil.

This wasn't the same as the Blasted Heath, though. Things weren't pressing against the veil to imprint on our reality. Something had moved this entire city into our reality from another. The creatures who had moved here had brought a piece of their home with them.

The city was too large for the basin that it rested in. It only made sense in that I hadn't expected it to make any sort of sense.

The geometry of the place was like everything else in the void and consisted of angles and dimensions that didn't exist in our reality. A mind less accustomed to the other realities would shatter under the pressures that such a sight would put on it. The ridiculously unnatural angles of the city gave way to shapes and patterns that also made sense when I studied them. I could make out spires and what I assumed to be buildings. Between them stretched pathways that were obviously roads.

The buildings themselves seemed honeycombed with holes in place of where I thought should be windows or some sort of viewing ports.

Over all of the foreign and incredibly familiar features that I recognized, the thing that stood out the most was how pristine the city was. The stone had no signs of wear or decay, even though it had been almost two decades since William had been there last and thousands of years since it had been supposedly abandoned. If the stone that the city had been constructed from had come from our planet, then I would have assumed it to be obsidian by how polished it was. Unfortunately, I was an archaeologist, among other things, and I knew of the hydration used in recognizing the age of obsidian and if this city was designed from the black volcanic glass, then it was recently pulled from the largest pit of obsidian in existence.

Hydration is the whitening of the edges of obsidian as it absorbs water over time. The buildings were completely black, showing none of the edging that should have come with age. If they were as old as I knew them to be, they were either not made of obsidian, or they were held in some sort of unaltered state of time.

How could I explain to Sebastian what I was seeing? It was foreign in idea and scope to anything that I had ever seen. Sebastian was even further from having any note of comparison than I was. How could I show him what I was seeing?

I opted against it, realizing that Sebastian would see it soon enough, and I wasn't expecting his mind to be capable of handling it.

"Keep circling," I managed. "We need to locate a place to attempt a landing."

Sebastian didn't like whatever shakiness or fear he might have heard in my voice. Maybe he heard the edges of insanity creeping back into my mind. I could feel the crawling oil-like feeling as it attempted to fill the void left by Olivia's leaving. I shook my head and tore my eyes away from the mesmerizing and alien sight.

My eyes closed tightly and my mind returning to its more sane state, the plane jostled up and down in the currents of air coming up from the basin. The jerking of the plane reminded me of my recently wounded shoulder that I had previously been doing everything in my power to forget. I seized it instead of ignoring it, allowing it to fill the places that the oily insanity had previously attempted to fill.

It was the trick of insanity that I had learned all too well. Insanity creeps into the cracks of your brain, so fill them with something else. It isn't a cure or a permanent fix, but it slows the oncoming darkness that will one day consume my entire being.

I hope that it does, anyway.

I reopened my eyes and began the search that I had told Sebastian was already underway. The city was so tightly packed, though, and I wasn't seeing any roadway or spacing that would provide the necessary length of runway to account for our momentum.

That led me to my second concern. While the buildings were all composed of stones that I was sure only looked like obsidian, I wasn't willing to bet against how sharp they would be when we hit them. Obsidian is sharper than the most freshly sharpened scalpels. If we were destined to crash through any of those structures, it was more than likely that the debris would slice us to ribbons.

"Do you see anything useful?" Sebastian asked, breaking me from my thoughts of imminent demise.

I shook my head and pulled my eyes away from the city again, choosing to focus on Sebastian while I spoke to him. "There are plenty of places to land, but none in which we would probably survive."

Sebastian nodded. I was sure that he had already come to a similar conclusion. A series of loud popping noises ran along our fuselage. Holes tore through my small window and the ceiling of the small cockpit. Sebastian pulled hard on the yoke and changed our direction with more speed than I was sure that the small collapsible plane was meant to endure.

"We've been spotted!" Sebastian was shouting.

Instead of shouting confirmation, I braved the cold air and looked through my broken window and back down upon the city. More loud pops filled our starboard wing with more holes, but instead of flinching, I watched for the flash of the large caliber gun that was being aimed at us.

There.

I saw the flash of the gunfire amid the buildings at the northern edge of the basin.

The dogs had long since sensed the panic that Sebastian and I were filled with and had begun whining. I had no doubt that they also felt trapped and the combination was making them bounce about.

I forgot my sore arm, and winced when I grabbed Sebastian's arm. In pain, I growled as I shouted, "Bring us down!"

"It's funny that you think I have a choice," Sebastian said.

I ignored him and added, "Wait until we get hit again and then bring us down fast." I added in hindsight, "Try not to kill us."

Sebastian's eyes were filled with incredulity as he asked me, "Where am I supposed to do this? Into the city or the side of a mountain?"

I shrugged because I really didn't know. This wasn't a plan, it was a reaction. I was dealing with the Nazi guns and not thinking much further than that. I doubted we had anything that was much further than that.

"If we succeed in destroying the city, we're probably going to die anyway. We might as well get it over with."

Fishing for any sanity that I might have left, Sebastian begged, "What about the dogs?"

"They're why I asked you to try and not kill us."

We didn't have long to wait. The gunner the Nazis were using was very skilled in his aerial combat skills. Machine gunfire tore through more of the plane and I heard one of the dogs let out a yelp, but they all stayed standing.

That was when Sebastian pushed the nose of the plane toward the city, and the first time that Sebastian laid his eyes upon such an alien sight.

Through heredity, Sebastian was more or less a creature from beyond the void, but heredity didn't carry much weight when your entire family shunned you from the education that should have been your birthright. He was raised as a one hundred percent human being, and his mental state was equivalent to it. It was one thing to worship and pray to beings on higher planes, but something else entirely to see something from that higher plane. It was beyond anything his mind could grasp.

His eyes went wide before they were suddenly absent of any recognizable facet of Sebastian. His brain had said goodbye to his body. Fear gripped my heart and I made a lunge for the yoke.

With a shudder and a shake of his head, Sebastian was slapping my hand away. "I'm not gone yet, old friend. At least let me crash the plane before you go taking things from me." He had a smile on his face, but it didn't reach all the way to his eyes. His eyes were filled with soul again, but it was damaged and shaky. I had seen men who had more fortitude than Sebastian be taken down by a much smaller glance than he had just had.

The yoke tore from Sebastian's grasp and the plane shuddered worse than before as it twisted down toward the city.

Sebastian wrestled with the yoke as he attempted to bring the plane back under his control.

Through gritted teeth, he said, "I don't think that crashing the plane will be that difficult." He shot me a quick glance. "That last shot killed us. I couldn't keep this plane in the air if I wanted to."

I figured as much, but hearing it was disheartening.

"I would like to add," Sebastian said, "that I very much want to."

Despite our situation, I laughed before shouting, "Let's ride this beast directly into Hell then!"

"Damn you, Andrew Doran!"

I spared a look at my friend. I was frustrated because I

couldn't do anything to help this situation. To be fair, it didn't look like Sebastian could do much either.

That was when I noticed the hole in Sebastian's jacket and the red oozing from it and over his seat.

I didn't say anything. We were most likely going to be dead in only moments, and letting him know that he had a potentially fatal wound was completely unnecessary. It wasn't going to be a gunshot that killed Sebastian Eliott.

Deciding on a new tactic, Sebastian pushed the yoke forward and the nose of the plane followed. I braced myself by grabbing the walls of the too-small cockpit and forced myself not to think about the still panic-filled dog breath that was hitting the side of my face.

As the nose dropped the madly configured city filled the front view. I could make out one lengthy bit of road that Sebastian seemed to be dragging the yoke toward, but I wasn't sure that the road was long enough to handle the speed that we were coming in at.

All the roads were basically bridges that spanned the path between the buildings and overlapped in an almost spiderweb fashion. I couldn't see the bottom of the bowl that the mountains formed and hoped that I never would.

The plane's port side wing clipped one of those bridges that crossed over the road that we were aiming for. The plane went into a spin and our fate was no longer being directed by Sebastian's hands.

We spun with such a speed that I didn't see the impact at all. I certainly felt it though. The jolt rammed up my spine and brought my head down and into what that tiny plane had for an instrument panel. Another jolt told me that we bounced. I braced myself enough by the second time to avoid another slam into the instrument panel.

Stars wracked my vision and I tried to focus but the inertia from the spin wasn't letting me do much of anything as it pressed me to the edge of the plane. I could only make out more and more black out of the window and assumed that it had to be the roadway we had landed on or an incoming wall.

The instrument panel crumpled inward. I didn't see it, but

I felt it as it crashed into my legs and drove me into my seat and the dogs. My head snapped forward and hit the edges of the instrument panel again.

The noise was like nothing that I had ever heard before. It was the tearing of metal and the shattering of glass-like stone. It was as if a train whistle was exploding in my head as metal sheared off in all directions.

The wall that we had hit stopped most of our spin and I could see well enough to see that our windows were all gone. The plane was still moving and was accompanied with the continuous rending of the metal as our plane slid across whatever the floors of this building were made of.

I knew that we had slid to a stop from the dogs leaping across my lap out of the plane more than from any sort of cessation of movement. The dogs yipped and disappeared quicker than I would have expected such terrified creatures to do.

Blood filled my vision and I touched my forehead to find that the instrument panel had sliced my brow. I mopped away as much of the blood out of my eyes as I could and tried to take in my foreign surroundings.

The nose of the plane faced away from any visible walls and only into the vast darkness that the dogs had disappeared into. Aside from that, I couldn't see much around the plane and what I could see was dark.

I tried to shift, but the impact with the other-worldly buildings had pushed the instrument panel further into the plane and pinned my legs. There was no pain in my legs and I felt around as much of them as I could reach before deciding that they were not broken, only pinned.

Wiping my forehead again, I turned to Sebastian who was unconscious and not moving.

"Sebastian! Wake up!" I was shouting as I reached over and shook him. When he didn't respond, I felt for a pulse in his neck. Although it was weak, he was still alive despite the crash and the gunshot wound.

I reached behind me and felt blindly for the scabbard that held my magical sword. After a moment of patting where the dogs had squeezed in behind us, my groping fingers finally located it.

Bringing it forward, I wedged it between my legs and used my right thigh as a fulcrum to bend the instrument panel away. I was hoping to free my legs, but was interrupted before I could even make the first attempt.

"I saved you from freezing to death and you're just going to leave me here ... to die?" His voice was weak, but it startled me from my work.

"Sebastian!" I replied, excited that he was conscious and not really taking note of his words. "Thank God! We need to get out of here."

He sneered at me. "This is what you do, isn't it? You use people to get where you need to go and then you discard them." He coughed and blood sprayed. Sebastian didn't bother to cover his mouth and it covered the yoke. "We are just trash to be thrown away by the great Dr. Andrew Doran."

What was he saying? Those words cut directly into my soul. I never saw my friends as a means to an end, but that doesn't mean that they weren't that by proxy. I feared every day that I was only using my friends to further my own crusade. I liked to think that I was nobler than that, but how does someone so noble manage to continue on with such a wake of death behind him?

Why else would I have allowed Nancy to accompany me? Her only value was in waking her father, and yet I didn't make her stay on the boat once that was accomplished. Was my subconscious such a horrible bastard that I had strung her along for an as-of-yet undetermined sacrifice?

How was I any better than the beasts that I put down?

Sebastian's words were my secret fear and they cut me so deeply that I was suddenly paralyzed with self-doubt...

...except, in this case the real lie was that I was sitting in the most alien city on Earth to destroy it.

The only priority in my heart was to save my companions. Everything else is secondary, including the destruction of the terrible city in those frozen mountains. I had decided this the moment that I woke up on the Arkatonic with that damned hole in my shoulder.

For another thing, those words of Sebastian's cut a little too well. It was as if he knew exactly the words that swam in my soul.

"Olivia."

Sebastian's possessed lips smiled at me. "Got it in one. I almost had you fooled."

I nodded, but answered, "Sebastian believes in me. He wouldn't expect the worst. Only my tumors pester me so incessantly."

"He's dying," she drawled. "I can feel his life draining away." Olivia reached around and poked at the hole in his side. "Another so-called friend that you've betrayed."

Anger filled my face, and it made me warm to see Olivia flinch at the sight. "You were not my friend." I twisted as much as my pinned legs would let me, turning to face the beast the resided in my friend's body. "You were using me. You never helped me, only yourself." I used the rage I gathered and applied pressure to the scabbard. My shoulder shouted at me and stars floated in my vision from the pain. The instrument panel shifted only marginally.

"Perhaps you're right," was Olivia's reply. "I owe you, so let me help you this time."

From somewhere on Sebastian's body, Olivia pulled a knife. "This time a friend's death will not be your fault."

Olivia plunged the knife into Sebastian's chest. The blade slid through coat and cloth as if they weren't there, and his smile wavered as the pain of the blade plunged into the chest she had borrowed.

She wheezed and her eyes were suddenly a flutter. In that flutter, I saw the return of Sebastian to his body. His smile transformed into a look of shock and surprise as more blood poured from his mouth. He looked down at his hand and saw it still holding the handle of the knife that protruded from his chest.

Sebastian's eyes spun to me and he tried to speak the confusion that had obviously filled every corner of his dying mind.

I was in shock and couldn't move. I only watched as he tried to ask what had happened. Finally, understanding filled his eyes and he very clearly mouthed the word, "Olivia."

Her name spurred me into action and I pried harder at the instrument panel to get it off my legs. I was frantic and the panel began to shift, but I noticed out of the corner of my eye that Sebastian was waving his hands about.

I stopped what I was doing and looked at my dying friend. He was smiling and gently moving his hand, palm toward me, in a calming gesture. He wheezed, "It ... is ... alright."

His hand fell, and Sebastian died.

I howled and howled, ignoring the dangers of broadcasting my language in this ancient city. The horrors of the dark be damned, my howls would guide my friend back to the living, or crush the already far away Olivia, or destroy this whole damned world.

It took only a few moments before I was able to bring myself back to any semblance of rational thought.

I did my best to ignore the fact that my friend was dead only inches from myself and poured my attention into moving the instrument panel off my legs. The stars returned to my eyes as my shoulder pain surged to the forefront of my mind. I didn't let it stop me and I could feel my shoulder tearing, but I didn't let it stop me. I needed to get out of that plane.

One more push and my legs were free enough for me to slide up in the seat and climb out through the non-existent window that the dogs had also escaped from. Before leaving the plane, I grabbed my scabbard and checked my pistol to make sure the accident hadn't destroyed the belt or the gun.

I thought about bringing the pack that I had filled before taking the sleds. In it were tools and papers regarding everything that William Dyer had described about this city.

I decided against it. I wouldn't need any of the tools and there wasn't anything in those papers that I hadn't already memorized. If my sword and gun wasn't going to be enough in the coming trials than nothing in that pack was going to prepare me any better.

That being said, I did take the compass, flares, and lighter from the pack.

As my feet touched the odd glass stone that made up the

entirety of the building that we had crashed into, I looked back at the still warm corpse of my friend.

It didn't feel right leaving him there, but I didn't know what else to do. He deserved a proper burial or at least a pyre, but I had no choice but to leave him behind.

If Strobel's men came looking for the crash site they would find it and they had no way of knowing that I'm still alive or that Sebastian wasn't alone. If I took his body, they would know to chase at least one person. Hopefully, those Nazi bastards would find Sebastian and assume the chase was over. They had no reason to think that I was still alive. Hopefully, my friend Sebastian could serve me one more time and help Strobel and his men to think that.

That thought led, inevitably, to Olivia's words. I was again using a friend.

I shook that thought from my mind as quickly as it entered it. The dead can't dictate the strategies of the living or we'd all start joining them. Right at that moment, I needed to survive if I was going to reach Leo and the Dyers. Olivia be damned.

I slid equipment around the cockpit to make it look like I hadn't been there, putting the pack that I had initially intended to bring with me in my seat as if Sebastian had placed it there.

Once I had completed staging the scene, I took out the compass. When we were crashing there had been a lot of spinning and inability to get my bearings. I still had a general idea of where I was, though, because we had gone down at a straight angle before we had begun our spin. It wasn't exact coordinates, but I had a general idea of where I was located within the city and I could remember which direction Strobel's trigger-happy Nazis had been shooting at us from.

If I was right, then Strobel and his men, and by proxy Leo and the Dyers, would be northwest of my current location. I turned toward the heading and decided that the dark tunnel it was aiming at would be my next step. I tore some cloth from the pack in the plane and wrapped it around my head to staunch the bleeding. All this I did while continuing to ignore my throbbing shoulder. It wasn't easy. It felt like everything in my shoulder was raw and grinding with every movement I made.

My shoulder and head trauma aside, I had already taken too much time in the crash and started off at a quick jog in the direction of the compass. The path continued to turn and curve at odd angles and I had to force myself to watch only the floor or ceiling, never the rest of the walls of the path.

I had run about one hundred yards and through six different bends when I realized that none of it made any sense. The most recent turn had caused the needle of the compass to bank left ninety degrees, but that wasn't all of it. The structure of the building and the turns that I had already taken, should have taken me outside of the building and onto one of the roadways or falling to my doom about thirty yards previously.

I wasn't surprised, but I was frustrated. The physics of the room was entirely different from the physics that I called home. The compass was right, but the building had taken me down a different angle, and I had become subjected to the linear movements of the building's plan.

It took a little bit more of head-spinning before I decided that following the compass was the only reliable means of heading in the direction that I wanted to go, even if it was going to randomly change course on me.

So, I randomly changed course with it.

The entire structure was ancient and the further I traveled into it, the more ancient the city looked. Walls were worn, and unlike the wind-polished stone outside the structure and near the plane crash, the building was falling apart.

There hadn't been a chance in our mid-air tumble to check out the other buildings, but I was willing to bet they were all in the same amount of disrepair. Yet, for ruins they looked newer than anything I had ever seen in my career. The Egyptian or Aztec Pyramids were in worse condition than anything I was seeing in those halls. Somehow, these ancient buildings had done more than stand the test of time. They had survived possibly millions of years and only looked a few centuries old.

Turning right ... or left ... I came across a corpse. In William's manuscript, he described creatures that were six feet tall and star-shaped with wings that fanned out. At full extension he said that the wingspan was at least seven feet.

I couldn't verify if the wingspan was seven feet or not, but the corpse was definitely six feet in height. If I wasn't in a hurry, I would have inspected the corpse longer. My quick glance confirmed everything that William had said, but my concern far surpassed my excitement. It was either incredibly well preserved or had died recently.

I hoped for the former, but doubted it.

I kept running, following the compass and trying to not let the different physics destroy my concentration. I saw carvings on the walls and statues sitting in the middle of the pathway. All the architecture and artwork was filled with the angular physics of the rest of the city, but it was also entirely organic-looking, as if it had been grown instead of carved.

Another turn in another impossible direction and I came upon a huge cavern. I flinched as the walls all lit up with some sort of inner luminescence. More drawings and carvings covered the walls and I began to recognize the scenes that Dyer had also described in his notes.

In his notes, and on those very walls, Nancy's father had described how the Elder Gods had been in a war for this very world.

They had spread into cities across our globe long before we were even on this planet. They developed primitive shoggoths, larger and without any specific shape, to be their slaves. These proto-shoggoths were also their warriors when the war finally came.

Cthulhu and his family came to the world after those cities had been established and chose to war for control. The war spanned the entire surface of the planet until the Elder Gods, losing ground, chose to withdraw to their last city with the last of the proto-shoggoths.

The war was over when the Mi-Go joined forces with Cthulhu and his brethren.

The Elder Gods retreated beneath the surface of their city and developed new shoggoths, the same shoggoths that would come to live in the shadows of our world today.

That city they went beneath was the city I was lost in right then.

Much of this I already knew from the Necronomicon as well as Dyer's notes. I probably could have translated the pictograms or whatever language the images were carved in if I were given enough time, but time was definitely something that I did not have.

I tore my eyes from the carvings and images and glanced at the compass. I used the reading to choose which of the many tunnels that shot off from the cavern I would take and resumed my run in that direction. I wasn't surprised when the lumination behind me blinked out as I left the large cavern.

Running down the corridor, the small amount of natural lighting that had been slipping between the cracks of this ancient city began to slim out. Suddenly, I was surrounded by too much dark to see the compass. I pulled a flare from my jacket and ignited it.

Keeping the arm holding the flare ahead of me, I glanced again at the compass and kept going.

I continued in that manner for what I could only guess at being about five hundred yards before the flare burned out.

As the hissing of the lit flare died along with its light, a clicking noise, like a cane tapping ice, echoed throughout the halls. Using only the last remains of the flare's life, I quickly found a wall and used it to guide me in the direction of the clicking noise. As the noise grew louder, and the flare grew dimmer, the darkness took on another quality altogether. It felt oily and organic as it began to press at the edges of the light, seeking to fill every corner of this long abandoned structure.

When the flare died, I continued onward allowing the wall to guide me. I would have used another flare or even my lighter to check the compass, but I figured that direction didn't even really matter at that point. That click-click-click had an ominous feeling with it that seemed attached to the darkness, and I didn't want to go any further leaving something like that at my back.

The clicking grew in intensity as I continued to feel my way around in the dark. Finally, when the clicking was so loud that I thought I was doing permanent damage to my ears, I risked lighting another flare.

The sight that sprang into existence before me, made all the more horrific by the red glow of that hissing flare, was possibly hundreds of giant white penguins. Their beaks were filled with gnarled and jagged teeth and those snapping beaks were the source of the clicking sound. They stood six feet tall and were snapping at anything that moved near them, including each other.

With the sudden ignition of the flare, their attentions all snapped toward me. I shook myself from my moment of frozen terror and threw the flare over their heads as I drew my .38.

As I took aim at the nearest freak, I noticed something that made me hesitate. The penguins all turned and rushed after the flare. I kept my gun trained on them but didn't fire. Instead, I took the moment to observe from the now darker side of the penguins.

They huddled around where the flare had dropped and snapped at it and each other. The flare managed a moment of bouncing around them as they snapped at it, burnt themselves and then snapped at it again. As I continued to watch, more and more snapping came from the edge of the large group as well. As they fought to get closer to the flare, one penguin would click louder than the rest and those nearest him would snap their terrifying jaws in that penguin's direction.

They were attacking the sounds. That was how I was able to get so close to them without the flare without them rushing me. When I had lit the flare and broken my silence I had given away my position with a constant hissing noise. These large albino penguins were blind and reacted to sound.

That must have been what the clicking was. They were using it to find their way through the tunnels.

The scientist in me wanted desperately to learn more about these creatures, but since I had come to the terrible city, I had become quite adept at silencing my inner scientist no matter how much he screamed. Instead, another idea popped into my head.

I scooped up some loose rubble and pulled from the scooped up amount a sizeable pebble. With a baseball pitch that would have made my ten year old self jealous, I threw it at a far wall on the edge of the penguins.

The resounding crack was nothing compared to the hissing,

but the penguins at the edge of the group turned immediately and waddled their way toward the new sound.

This was going to be very useful.

The flare still had a lot of life left to it, so I decided to see exactly how deep this herd of monster penguins went.

I moved as quietly as I could between them as they pushed and snapped at each other. I tried to stay low and as far from their beaks as I could, but they stretched the entirety of the hall and as I moved through them and past the flare, the darkness made it easier and easier to crash directly into one of them.

I managed to get through with a minimal number of bites at me and my jacket was tattered around my shoulders. On the other side of them, I continued forward until the sound of their click-click-click began to subside. Once I felt that I was far enough away, I pulled my lighter from my pocket and took a look at the compass. I was still moving in the right direction, but I had already traveled for so long that I was no longer sure if distance even mattered.

I should have seen some sign of the Strobel and his men. Uncertainty and worry were beginning to set in.

I hadn't traveled over any of those walkways that Sebastian and I had seen on the way into the city. Yet, I had traveled farther than should have been possible within this one building. I was either moving between the buildings by another method, or this one building was incredibly larger than it should have been. I hoped that I was traveling between the buildings somehow, because the other option meant that I was never going to find my way out or to the Germans.

Finding my strength, I pushed onward. I made sure not to get too far ahead without making some noise to bring my new friends along with me. Their constant clicking remained a steady hum in the back of my mind as I continued forward. We continued that way for another hour before I finally found the damned Nazis.

I heard them before I saw them. The steady clicking was joined by the more recognizable hum and whine of machinery. I put away my compass and lighter and followed that noise until I found its source.

Another large cavern, much like the first one that I had come across, was filled with generators, machinery, lighting, and German soldiers. There was also a lot of weaponry.

This cavern was twice the size of the first one that I had found and had pillars reaching toward the decorated ceiling. It still had that organic look and for some reason the walls didn't light up as the previous cavern's had. Only half of the pillars were still standing, the rest were scattered around the room in large piles of rubble. Strobel's men weren't worried about anyone coming after them, because they hadn't placed much in the way of guards at the tunnel entrance that I had come from.

One man stood guard, but he was facing the cavern itself and drinking with another soldier. Sneaking past them was simple.

From there, I maneuvered between the piles of rubble and machinery around the edge of the cavern. I wasn't only avoiding the large army, I was also conducting reconnaissance.

I saw a lot of Nazi soldiers that were nothing like the first two I had come across. Fear was permeating their mindsets. Several of the soldiers were laid out on stretchers with what looked like burns and bite marks. They had come across something in their migrating through the caverns.

Finally, I found my companions. They were near the opposite end of the cavern from where I had entered. Together they were sitting on the floor of the cavern against a fallen pillar. Leo's face was swollen and I took that to mean that, in pure Leo fashion, he couldn't keep his mouth shut.

Nancy was lying with her head on her father's lap. Her eyes were wide open and staring off at nothing. William had his journal and my hopes lifted.

William was panning through it, but unlike on the boat, his brow wasn't furrowed with confusion. Instead, he was skimming pages and then moving on to the next.

He was reading it.

Standing over them, fear creasing their foreheads, were two guards. They were both standing closer to Leo and had their guns drawn.

Leo, Nancy, and her father all had their hands tied with a

rope connecting each of them at the wrists. The end of the rope was being held by one of the guards.

Considering my recon completed, I made the painstakingly slow return back to where I had entered the cavern. On my way there, I came across a smaller hole in the wall of the cavern that held a tunnel only slightly larger than myself. I filed that useful information away for later and kept moving until I was almost all the way back to my new albino allies.

Once I had reached them, I pulled out the last flare and lit it.

Chapter 10: The Tunnels

The only warning that any of Strobel's men received came in the form of a bouncing flare that was shooting sparks as it slid past their feet.

Their first thoughts came in the form of multiple shouts of *"Bombe! Bombe!"*

I was watching from the shadows of the hall as one of the Nazis began laughing and picked it up, waving it around. As he continued laughing, one of his fellow soldiers turned to look down the tunnel, peering into the darkness.

He looked right at me and didn't even see me.

How could he see me, when hundreds of six foot tall, carnivorous, albino penguins waddled with an amazing speed into the cavern after their favorite toy flare.

Clicking filled the entire cavern with so much noise that the screams of the soldiers became drowned out by it. I covered my ears and ran between my new allies and back along the path that led to my companions.

Gunfire mixed with the clicks and I took a moment to look at how the battle was going.

It was bloody. The soldiers had never encountered anything like these blindly biting and snapping penguins. Gunfire rang out, but panic made many of the shots either go wide or only hit the penguins in the torso. Torso shots would kill the beasts, but anyone who's ever hunted knew that it would only piss them off first. Enraged, the penguins bit at anything that made a sound. Mostly that included soldiers, but some infighting among the penguins was also happening.

The Penguin Menace was making quick work of the first

round of soldiers. Beaks tore away limbs and buried themselves into chests. One large beak wrapped directly around the neck of one soldier who was trying to shoot a penguin off his arm. In one powerful squeeze, his head came off. His death didn't stop their lunges, though and the two penguins worked in concert to tear him to shreds.

The first wave of Strobel's men was taken by surprise, but the second had time to get over their shock and open fire. Unfortunately, their own men acted as shields and protected many of the penguins, but many penguins also died.

I had no doubt that the Germans would come out as the victors, but I wasn't sure about how long it would take or how many of them would die in the process. I tore my eyes away and returned to hunting for my friends.

As I moved, bullets flew over my cover and into the wall behind me. I spared a quick glance and realized I had nothing to fear. The penguins were advancing nearly as much as I was, and none of the guns had been aimed at me.

In German, I heard someone shout, "All at once now!" I recognized Strobel's voice immediately and moved faster. If he was organizing his soldiers than the battle would be over soon.

My companions were right where I left them. They were still seated, but that was the doing of the guards. It was obvious that they were anxious to see what was going on.

William was still frantically reading the journal while his daughter and Leo strained their necks to watch the fight. Their guards were also watching the battle, but kept glancing down at Leo.

My friend must have given them quite the hard time.

I stood and drew my pistol. Firing two rapid shots, I dropped both of the guards before they could turn in my direction. Then I drew my sword and moved to cut the ropes.

Faster than I would have anticipated, Leo lunged at my waist. His tackle knocked the wind out of me and knocked me to the ground. Rope still around his hands, Leo straddled me and began beating on my already damaged head.

His blows rained down on me and he shouted words that I assumed were in French, but I was too busy getting beat to catch.

Between the abrupt tackle and my wounded shoulder I was incapable of fighting him off, and assumed I would be dead before I could finish rescuing my friend.

Then, as quickly as it had happened, it was over.

Leo was pulled off me by William and his daughter and dragged a few feet away. Holding their own ropes tight, they held him in place.

"What the hell was that about?" I demanded when I had caught my breath.

"Monster!" Leo howled in English. He struggled against his captors again, but they held him tight.

Over the strain of holding Leo still, Nancy said, "We saw you die." She grunted. "This place is filled with monsters. Are you one?"

I shook my head and pulled open my jacket over my shoulder. I grunted in pain as I did it. The bandage had more than soaked through and the jacket was sticking to the bloody mess. "Strobel shot me in the shoulder." I pulled the coat back on and scooped up my sword and pistol from the cavern floor. "Sebastian saved me after he heard the gunshot."

Leo calmed almost instantly. "The Arkatonic?"

I shook my head.

Nancy added, "Sebastian?"

I shook my head again and added, "Most of his men survived."

It wasn't the time to tell them about Olivia's part in killing Sebastian. The clicking had become less pronounced and the gunfire had slowed. We needed to get moving.

I cut the ropes and helped William gather his notes and the journal.

Leo slapped me on my good arm and was smiling.

"I knew that death would not hold you for long."

I indicated my shoulder and replied, "Not for lack of trying."

My friend laughed and then went to the dead guards to gather their weapons. Leo checked his machine gun and then handed the other to Nancy. He tried to show her how to use it, but she shrugged him off and checked the chamber without help.

We took off back the way that I had come with myself in the lead. As we moved, I risked a peek at the battle and noted that most of my penguin army was dead. They had taken a lot of the Nazi soldiers with them, but not nearly enough. Their purpose had been to cause a distraction, but I was a little disappointed that they hadn't eliminated the entire German forces.

We came to the person-sized tunnel that I had noticed earlier and I directed everyone inside, with me taking up the rear in case anyone saw us go in.

Somewhere around thirty yards into the tight tunnel, William began to panic.

"Move, move, move. We need to go back. We can't be here!" His words were stringing together so quickly that I couldn't hear what he was saying. I had to ask Nancy, who was directly between her father and myself, what it was that he was saying.

She added, "He says that these are the tunnels reserved for the servants to move around the city." Her face paled as she realized what that meant.

"Why should that matter?" Leo said loudly from the front of our troupe.

I had been careless and stupid, and that realization presented itself as rage. I slapped the stone wall solidly, sending a wave of pain from my wounded shoulder that threatened me with nausea. William had known right away and I should have consulted with him about these tunnels before we dove in.

"It matters," I answered trying to temper the frustration in my voice, "because the Elder Things that lived here were served by shoggoths!" The last word came out in a hiss.

Leo had traveled with me long enough to know what a shoggoth was and his face lit up with understanding before a flash of fear passed over his swollen eyes.

Leo turned to William immediately and began talking him down. Panic in an enclosed space that could possibly be closed off by ancient proto-shoggoths wasn't going to help us survive. After a few moments, William quieted, but his panic was still evident.

"What did he tell him?" I asked Nancy.

Nancy frowned. "Leo said that we don't know that any

shoggoths are still around and using these tunnels. He said that going forward was only probably going to kill us, but going backward was definitely going to kill us."

It was hard to argue with that logic.

Our team continued down the tunnel and through several turns with minimal visibility. At one point, I passed my lighter up to Leo so that he could have some sort of warning before any shoggoths were right on top of us. There were offshoots and other tunnels that intersected with the one that we were using, but we stayed true to that one, hoping that at a later time we might be able to map out where we were and where we would need to go. We didn't hold strong to that hope as we had all experienced the backwards physics of the city, but we didn't want to make anything harder on ourselves than it had to be.

Finally, our tunnel opened up into a smaller room, nothing like the two caverns that we had previously seen. This room was still covered in the smooth-as-glass stone, but the little light that there was had a red hue to it. Whereas the caverns had been circular, this room was perfectly square and about the size of my office back in Miskatonic. Two large statues on plinths had made up the center at one point, but all that remained of the statues were chunks of stone surrounding the plinths. The plinths themselves were around the length of a person wide and long and stood shoulder height on me.

The panic and the tight quarters left our party catching their breath. Leo inspected the rest of the room while I put my head back into the tunnel we had just left. I needed to know if we were being followed by Nazis, stray penguins, or proto-shoggoths. Although, I was sure that we wouldn't know the proto-shoggoths were near until they were on us.

I held my breath as I listened and stood there like that for a full thirty seconds before letting my breath go again. I turned back toward the group.

"I don't think that we were followed."

Nancy's shoulders visibly sagged and her father quickly fell to the floor between the plinths and returned to poring over his journal.

Leo came up to me, "There is only one other entrance to this place and it is the same size as the tunnel that we left. It is a fair bet that this place was only used by the shoggoths."

That didn't sit well with me, but I was willing to push it to the back of my mind for the moment. "Well, I figure that we won't have to worry about the shoggoths for now and the Germans haven't picked up on us yet. I suggest that we rest." Then a thought occurred to me. "But no one sleeps!" I said it a little louder than I needed to, but it got the message across. I calmed down as I added, "In case we need to move."

Leo saw past my outburst and lowered his voice so that the Dyers couldn't hear what he was saying. "You saw her again?"

I nodded. "Sebastian and I flew here. It was the only reason I found you as soon as I did."

Leo's eyes lit up. "They were shooting at you."

I nodded again. "We crashed and Sebastian had been hit. When he blacked out, Olivia was there." I shook my head. "He didn't make it."

Understanding and sympathy filled Leo's expression. "I am sorry. He was a good friend."

"Yes," I agreed. "And another one lost in my foolish crusade."

Leo gave me a half-grin. "All crusades are foolish until they bring results. Let us bring this one to a close so that his death isn't equally as foolish."

He stepped away from me and took a seat across from the Dyers at the other plinth. I joined him with the Dyers sitting against one plinth and us facing them sitting at the other plinth.

I waved a hand at William and asked, "What is this all about? He couldn't read that damned book yesterday."

Leo nodded. "You are not the only one who has been through much. We marched for half of a day before we finally reached trucks. It was at that point that they decided that killing me would be easier. My only value would be as a hostage against you, and you were dead."

Nancy interrupted. "Until I spoke up. I told them that he had become invaluable to father in the translation of the journal."

Leo nodded. "Instead of killing me, they beat me to find out how true it was. I spouted things that I had heard you say about the void. It seemed to be convincing enough. They beat me for another handful of minutes before Strobel demanded that they put me in the truck." He didn't say it with any pain in his face, only as a fact. Leo was a soldier and knew that sometimes that meant taking an ass-kicking.

"We arrived at the city and somehow they began unloading explosives." Leo frowned. "It was as if they knew right where to hit the mountain. The explosion opened up a tunnel that led directly into the city."

William looked up from his journal then. "That would be my fault. In my original document, I explained the exact location of where tunnels ran through the mountain. Danforth found an entire map. I included that."

I shook my head. "Then it wasn't your fault. It was Brandon Smythe's fault. He's the one who gave everything that you left at Miskatonic to the Germans."

That didn't seem to change the guilt-ridden look on William's face, but he dropped the subject and put his nose back into the journal.

Leo picked the story back up. "It didn't take long for us to figure out that they are definitely looking for some sort of armory or weapons cache." Leo waved his hand at William. "He still couldn't read the journal when we finally made it into the city. It wasn't until we reached what Dyer kept calling the Central Commons that the journal finally made itself clear to him."

William looked up again. "The Central Commons is the common area for the entire city. It was by sheer luck that we found it."

"What is it?" I begged.

"The Central Commons is where all of the maps of the city are. Instead of histories written all over the walls, maps and alien languages cover every inch of that massive place," William said. "Once I was in there, something…" he hesitated, "clicked … and I was able to read the journal again." It was William's turn to frown, "Although, it turns out that while I was here previously, I had written the entire thing in my own code. I have been deciphering it since."

"And what does it say?" I demanded.

William's eyes grew wide. "For one, it showed me that those smaller tunnels are for those beastly shoggoths. They have no solid mass and are therefore able to squeeze into much smaller tunnels than their barrel-shaped masters." He calmed back down. "For another, it has shown me how to navigate this place. I'm fairly certain that I could find the armory that the Nazis are looking for."

"Good," I said. "You're going to take us there."

"What?" William said. "Are you just another war monger like our German enemies?"

I shook my head, but before I could reply, Leo answered for me. "If you are going to destroy a city, you need a very big bomb. Where would you hide a big bomb, Dr. Dyer?"

Realizing his point. William lowered his head back into his journal and kept scribbling notes.

Leo looked at me with a smile. "We might actually pull this off."

I smiled and put false bravado behind my words. "Of course! I never had any doubts."

Something crossed my mind then. "If there's an entire map room, why did you need the journal to navigate us? Can't the Germans still find the armory?"

William shook his head. "The maps were extradimensional. Our minds cannot retain them after we have seen them." He held up his journal, "That is why I wrote this, but I also wrote this to explain the hazards that we face."

"Hazards?" I asked. "Like the shoggoths?"

William shook his head. "No. Environmental hazards. A map room that the mind can't hold onto isn't the only alien thing in this city. We are only human and there are environmental conditions that the Elder Things were more adept at handling than we are."

I frowned, "A lot of them?"

William smiled. "No need to worry, Andrew. I have it all mapped out here. There are work-arounds for most of them."

I accepted William's statement as truth and decided to rest my head against the plinth for a moment. Before it could touch the cold and smooth stone, I decided to ask Leo, quietly, how

Nancy and William had been holding up.

"Nancy is our little soldier. I have been very impressed by her." On my encouragement, Leo continued. "I made an early attempt to escape and she took out two of the German soldiers by herself."

I was also impressed and whispered as much.

"And her father?"

Leo frowned. "Obsessed. Once we entered the Central Commons his nose was in that journal of his and he only came up when he needed air." Leo smirked at his own joke.

His smile turned serious. "Blowing up the city is a good plan. With Dyer we could even make it work, but what about after? How do you plan to get us away with our boat sunk and a Nazi sub guarding the waters?"

I couldn't even bring myself to smile as I said, "The same way we always escape: with a whole lot of luck."

Leo hung his head and began to laugh quietly. "Let us hope that our luck never runs out."

I agreed with him and the following silence made me realize something.

Nancy hadn't said anything in quite a while.

I turned my eyes toward her and saw her, with her head on her father's lap. Her eyes were wide open and staring at me.

She was smiling.

Leo noticed her at the same time I did. "Is everything alright, Nancy?"

"That isn't Nancy." I replied.

At some point in the last few minutes Nancy had fallen asleep.

Leo realized what I was saying and brought his pistol up and took aim on Nancy. William finally took notice and began to demand what was going on when Nancy sat straight up.

I put my hand on Leo's arm and lowered his gun. "How can we help you, Olivia?"

Olivia, in her Nancy suit, shook her head. "How can I help you?"

She slowly raised her own pistol and aimed it at Leo and then her father and then at me. "All of this dead weight is slowing us down!" She was spitting as she spoke. "Anyone can read that damned journal now and Leo looks like he lost a fight with a baseball bat! Let me help you again!"

William looked at his daughter. He didn't understand what was going on.

It was then that he said the words that I hoped he would never say again. "Nancy, what are you doing?" Stress filled his face and his confusion was turning to fear. "Put down the gun, my girl!"

Olivia made a mocking hurt face, "Maybe I wouldn't be holding a gun at all if my daddy hadn't run away from home."

William's fear is replaced with concern. "That wasn't my choice, Nancy. You know that."

"Blah, blah, blah, bang!" Olivia said, and then shot William in the throat.

Surprise filled William's eyes as he slumped over.

Leo leaped up and at her quicker than I could, but Olivia was faster and spun around with her pistol. Three more gunshots took Leo in the gut and he collapsed between Olivia and me.

I was screaming and my own pistol was up and aimed at Nancy's body before I realized what I was even doing. I halted myself from shooting her and instead leapt at Olivia.

But not physically.

On instinct, I left my body and jumped at my insanity. As I came at her I noticed that I wasn't the only one. She had summoned the Night Gaunt to return her to the Dream Lands.

The Night Gaunt got to her before I did, but I still got to her. As she started to rise into the aether, I gripped her around the waist and jerked down with all of my spiritual strength.

Together the three of us, the Night Gaunt, Olivia, and I, all fell to the floor.

Olivia kicked me in the face before I could get up.

"My world, my rules, Doran!" She kicked me again. "We could have been happy together!" She was screaming. Another kick came at my face. "What did you hope to accomplish by coming here?"

I sat up before she could kick me again and said, "I just wanted to release your pet."

The guttural language of the Night Watchers erupted from my mouth as I cast a spell that Olivia never took the time to learn.

The Night Gaunt's head jerked toward me at the sound of those words. Its blind gaze looked right at me before jerking back toward Olivia. Olivia's eyes went wide with realization. She barked the only guttural command that she had ever learned. It was the same phrase that I had taught to the Ancient Child, but her words had no effect this time.

The Night Gaunt, now freed from her control and resenting the claim of ownership that Olivia had placed over it, lunged at her.

She swung her arms and barked other magical phrases she had learned while riding shotgun in my brain, but nothing stopped her attacker as it batted her hands aside and tore into her neck with its fierce claws. As her neck ripped, her screams went quiet.

It was quite different to see the death of this completely spiritual being than it was to see William die.

Instead of bleeding from her wounds, each new wound aged her. In seconds, she looked over a hundred years old and her flesh just began falling off.

I enjoyed every moment of her death, watching with a sadistic glee that I hadn't realized myself capable of.

When not even dust remained of Olivia, the Night Gaunt turned toward me. I could tell that it was sizing me up, preparing to make an attack, but I did nothing.

Night Gaunts are intelligent creatures and this one was no exception. It might have been the hands that destroyed Olivia, but I was the one who had been the victor in that battle. Instead of lunging at me, it leapt straight up and vanished into the nothingness.

I returned to my body and moved to Leo's side. He was still gasping and spitting blood with each breath.

"You damned idiot!" I shouted at him. "I told you to ignore her."

Leo spit blood. "She ... killed Dyer."

I slapped my hand on the floor in anger. "And you, dammit!"

Suddenly Nancy was conscious again. Her eyes fell on Leo and I first and she was by our side in seconds. "What happened? Oh my God! What happened?" Her head spun around and her eyes found her father before I could say anything. Her screams were incomprehensible.

Finally, she's just repeating through tears as she hugged her father's dead form to her chest, "What happened?"

Leo shook his head at me and I understood what he meant. "The Nazis found us. I was able to push them back, but they got us." I hugged her to me, pulling her off her father. "Nancy, I am so sorry. I am so very sorry." I said those words, but I couldn't stop thinking about how much Olivia's gunshots had alerted everyone in the city to our current location. "Nancy, we need to get out of here. They are going to be coming back."

She pulled away from me then and fell on top of her father, sobbing into his blood soaked shirt.

Leo tried to sit up, but spat up a lot more blood. He was dying and it wasn't going to be long.

"Sit still, idiot." I told my friend. "I am going to try something."

I reached into the void and forced it through my body and into my hands which were hovering over Leo's wounds. Using my will, I tried to shape the power and then released it.

The pain on Leo's face was suddenly gone and his breathing became much steadier.

"What did you do?" Leo asked.

I frowned as I answered, "I didn't save you, if that's what you're asking." I helped him to his feet. "That is a fatal wound and gut shots don't heal."

"If I am not healed, then why do I feel better?" Leo asked.

"Take a look." I said, waving my hand at his stomach.

Leo unzipped his jacket and pulled up his shirt. Underneath, his flesh was pale and stained with his blood. Wiping away as much as he could, he saw that he still had the three bullet holes and they were still leaking blood, but not nearly as fast as they had been previously.

"I took away the pain and slowed your death. We still have a war to win."

Leo frowned but nodded. "I am unsure how I feel about this."

I explained, "We had two options. Either you die and leave us to find this armory by ourselves with monsters and a large collection of Nazis hunting us, or I could give you a chance to save our lives, the world, and to take the fight one last time to the Nazis. Did I guess wrong in what my friend in arms would prefer?"

Leo gave me half of a grin. "No, but I still would have preferred a discussion."

"Duly noted." I replied. Looking at Nancy, I added. "Don't tell her. I don't want her thinking that I could save her father. That kind of false hope would destroy her." Leo nodded in reply.

I pulled Nancy away from her father again. "Nancy, we have to go. We can't stay here."

"We can't leave him!"

I slapped her. Hard. "Nancy, he would not want you to die. Not here. Not now. Not ever. We must go."

"What am I supposed to do?"

Leo stepped forward and handed Nancy her father's journal.

"We need you to read your father's code for us. We need you to take us to the armory."

Nancy pulled the journal from Leo's hands but kept staring at his blood-stained coat. "I thought he were hurt?"

Leo smiled, "It was only a graze. I have a tendency to be overly dramatic."

Chapter 11: The Madness

We moved at a slower pace than we had through the first proto-shoggoth tunnels. Leo's pain might have been suppressed, but the damage to his abdomen was still there. I could see the frustration in his face whenever the glow from the lighter flashed across him.

I led the charge with Leo guarding our flank. Nancy was between us and was another reason for our slow progression. It wasn't that her grief was slowing her, although I wouldn't fault her if it was. Instead, she had buried her grief under the weight of her new responsibility with the journal.

So far, Nancy had been able to read the markings in the proto-shoggoth's tunnels and that had been the first sign that we were on the right path. Leo and I had never noticed the marks the first time we had moved through the tunnels. They looked nothing like the markings throughout the rest of the city. Instead, these were cuts in the walls, slashes that looked similar to Celtic Ogham. I figured that the proto-shoggoths must have needed their own slave language. Similar incidents had been reported throughout all of human history, and the parallels to the proto-shoggoths were both interesting and terrifying at the same time.

Before we could dive back into the tunnels, Nancy had needed to read her father's notes and locate where he thought the armory would be. After that, we knew the general direction that we needed to go. Periodically, Nancy would see something on the walls that would cause her to shout or panic and we would switch direction without asking her why. I desperately wanted to know why. I had an ominous feeling that Strobel was also moving in the correct direction, and I didn't want to waste the time learning the language of the proto-shoggoth or the dangers that their world might have presented to us, no matter how much I wanted to.

"This place makes no sense," Leo said as we took another turn. "My sense of direction is very good, and we should be well outside of the mountains by now."

I nodded without looking back at the Frenchman. "This entire place exists in our reality, but not fully a part of it. It's part of the void, but on the wrong side of the veil."

Leo asked, "What about the roads and separate buildings? We have seen none of those since we entered."

"I think," I answered, "that those were there as part of our understanding. We expected to see an alien city, so we saw an alien city."

"What does that even mean?" Leo sounded even more frustrated.

Nancy halted in her steps, lifted her free hand and wiggled her fingers. "It's magic. Now shut up, I'm trying to concentrate."

I didn't have to see Leo's face to see the frown that he was most definitely wearing.

We exited that proto-shoggoth tunnel into a room that spanned at least a hundred yards across and up. I forced my mind to pull away from examining, yet again, the complete departure from physics and walked into the room.

The room, for all of its vastness, was completely empty. At the far end, I could see another entrance similar to the one that we had just walked through. The floor was the big departure from the rest of the city. It was covered with large grooves and seams that spanned the entirety of the room. It was an intricate pattern that interweaved across the room, creating hexagonal shapes that fit together and overlapped each other. It was as mesmerizing as the most beautiful piece of art, and the more I looked at it the more obsessed I became with trying to understand it.

With considerable effort, I regained my senses and turned to see that both Nancy and Leo had fallen under the control of the hypnotic floor.

I shook both of my friends until their glazed look vanished. Leo was easier to bring back than Nancy had been, but after our time in the Blasted Heath I had expected as much.

"What is this?" I asked Nancy.

She looked at me with a moment of confusion. I am normally the one with the answers, but this time I needed her expertise with her father's journal. This was beyond me.

"This is what father called 'The Pit.'" she pointed across the room to the other entrance. "The armory is through that tunnel, but crossing this room is something that humans shouldn't be able to do."

"Why not?" Leo asked.

She waved her hand at the floor, and as her eyes passed over it they started to glaze. I snapped my fingers and Nancy was back with us.

"The floor has three different radiations that grow with intensity the closer we get to that door. It's a type of defense against the lesser creatures entering."

"Radiations?" I asked.

Nancy nodded. "Not like what we know as radiation, but something from beyond that is emitted by whatever is under the floor."

"That's wonderful," I said. "What do they do?"

She waved her hand again. "I do not know." Nancy gulped as she thought of William. "My father knew that they existed and he knew the location of the armory, but he didn't know what these radiations are supposed to do."

"It's alright, though, isn't it?" Leo asked. "Humans cannot pass 'The Pit,' so the Nazis have lost and we do not need to destroy the city."

I shook my head and turned toward him. "You have fought enough of the Nazis in the last few years to know that they are not all human. This fight is far from over."

He stomped his foot on the floor that kept calling for my attention. "Than what can we do?"

Leo was right, for all of our otherworldly exploits, we were still only human.

"Couldn't you shield our minds," Nancy asked. "Like you

did when father and I were unconscious in the woods."

"That wasn't a shield, I just made us harder to see..." An idea began to form in my mind. "I could try something else, though."

My hesitancy to explain frustrated Leo. "What? What could you do?"

"I could shield your minds with a different spell. I could take another mind, or presence, and blanket it over your minds."

"No," Leo said immediately understanding my meaning.

"Why not?" Nancy asked.

Leo shook his head and jabbed a finger in my direction. "He means he would take the brunt of the attack meant for us. It would be his mind that he put in front of our own."

"It could work, Leo." I argued. "My mind has shown to have an amazing durability under the powers of the void." Leo was shaking his head. I pointed at his stomach. "Dammit, Leo! Anything to stop them!"

Leo stopped and looked at the waist of his coat. It was still wet with his slowly leaking blood. "Then use my mind as the shield."

"I can't," I answered. "I can't manipulate someone else's mind as easily as I can my own. It would be like trying to drive your truck from the outside. It can't be done."

He stomped around for another minute or so, cursing in French, and I couldn't blame him. He had accepted his death knowing that his friends had the potential to live on because of his sacrifice. Now he was seeing that his hopes were not necessarily fact.

I looked to Nancy during Leo's frustrated tantrum and saw that she was only staring blankly at the tunnel from which we had come. It wasn't the floor's doing. She had seen enough death and she was only waiting for us to make the decision so that we could continue. Nancy no longer cared.

Leo stomped up to me and thrust his index finger at my face. "Fine! What do you need from us?"

I pulled them both in close to me, one on each side, and placed my hands on their foreheads.

"All you need to do is walk to the door. If my hand starts to slip, grab it and hold it on your forehead. You will be walking and guiding me, my feet will just be going through the motions."

They both nodded and I gathered my will. Mixing my concentration with the energy of the void, I expanded my consciousness to include them both. I couldn't read their thoughts or anything to that nature. It was more like I could sense a mild empathy.

Nancy was a storm of emotion that rolled just under the surface. There was so much going on in her emotions that it came across as a quiet static to me.

I almost couldn't sense Leo. It took me a while to recognize that the small sadness I felt wasn't my own. Leo didn't want to die, and I didn't blame him.

"Walk," was all that I said that started our troop in motion.

Both of my friends began to march slowly across 'The Pit.' It didn't take a genius to know where the name came from. The further in we went, and with three people's worth of radiation hitting me, all that I wanted to do was crawl into the floor. I wanted to fall into its embrace and feel the warmth of … of…

Something must have happened because I felt a sudden jolt as I was hauled upward. I must have started to sag to the floor.

My floor. That beautiful floor. It knew me like no one had ever known me. Not my parents, long destroyed in their own nightmares. Not Leo, my friend and ally in this war who I had led to his death. Not Olivia, who had even been a part of my very soul.

Olivia who I had betrayed.

What vile creature was I that I had betrayed the only being in existence who could possibly understand everything that I…

My hand was grasped and thrust against something cold and clammy. It snapped me back to my mind quickly enough to realize that I had been falling into a pit of despair.

Fire.

Fire was suddenly in my mind. It raged inside and tore at my every thought. My throat was in unknowable agony and somewhere in the back of my mind I knew that it was because I was screaming. So much pain. If only I could let it out. Let it out. Let it out. Let it out. Let it out.

Something had grabbed my other hand. It was slapping it. I had to get away. Fight this thing. Always fight. Fighting will free me. Break me from the fire. The fire. In my head. The fire that looked like...

Terror. Oily black horrors from the ends of time. Slimy tendrils of soul-staining evil wrapped around each of my hands and tearing at my flesh. As my flesh sloughed from my bones the putrid oily things consumed it with their mouths that were nothing like mouths. It screamed with an alien voice but I knew the words. *Andrew Doran must be ended.* I wanted to help them. What was this Andrew Doran that had slowed my embrace of the terror? The oily black horrors that had burrowed deep within my...

A slap. Another slap. What had I done to deserve the slaps? This time it was on my face. I grasped at it and realized that my hands were free. Whatever had been holding them had finally released me. I could open my eyes now. I could fight.

My eyes opened and they fell upon a girl. I lunged at her, but again I was grabbed. This time from behind. I bucked and kicked until I knew what this thing in front of me was. This girl.

She was Nancy.

I calmed and fought to remember why she was Nancy. She was Nancy because she was in Dyer's office. Yig cultists had chased us until we had found Dyer ... Dyer... Her father. William Dyer.

Suddenly, my mind was my own again and I told Leo as much. When he finally believed me, he let me go and I sagged with my eyes closed as I spoke.

"Where are we?"

Leo answered. "We have moved about thirty yards into the new tunnel. Your trick worked. Nancy and I didn't feel a thing." He placed a hand on my shoulder. "If you are alright to continue, you can open your eyes. We have gone around a corner and 'The Pit' is well out of sight."

I grabbed at the lighter from Nancy, flicked it on, and waved it about.

"How close are we?"

She shook her head. "I don't know. It will be at the end of this tunnel."

"I think that a more pressing question," Leo said, "is how are we going to ever leave this place? Now we have added 'The Pit' to the list of things between us and returning home."

That list included an army of Nazis, a Nazi submarine, an ocean, and no ship to sail it with.

I shook my head. "We will worry about that later. Not now, when we're so close." I nodded to Nancy and handed her back the lighter. "After you, m'lady."

She started off moving deeper into the tunnel. I started to follow but as I passed Leo he grabbed my arm.

"Start thinking about how you're getting home. If not for your sake, then for hers. She didn't ask for any of this. She only wanted to find her father, and now he's dead."

I pulled from his grip. "Don't you think I know that?" Olivia's words echoed again through my mind. "My initial plan had included the boat and killing a lot of Nazis. I didn't want her getting mixed up in all of this, but now that we're here the only viable plan is to move forward. I'll figure this out."

"You had better." Leo returned before setting off after Nancy.

We walked another mile or so when Nancy stopped.

Even with the lighter in her hand, my thoughts were so focused on how I would get us out of there that I still crashed into her and Leo.

"Why did we stop?" I was confused because I didn't see anything, but also excited because there are very few reasons why she would have stopped.

"Because we're here ... and because of that." Nancy held the lighter out in front of her and a large and decorated wall came into light.

Except that it wasn't a wall at all. A seam ran down the middle. It was so smooth that it almost wasn't visible in the lighter light. I stepped in front of Nancy and ran my hand over the door.

It was carved with geometric shapes that were mostly recognizable, but followed no specific pattern that I could see. After I examined the door, I turned to Nancy and raised an eyebrow.

"If it's a language, then I can't read it." She answered my unasked question.

I couldn't read it either, so I was willing to bet against it being any sort of language. As I felt more around the corners and curves of the door I decided that it must be artistic over functional.

"How do we open it?" Leo asked.

I shrugged. Using my fingernails, I tried to grab at the seam, but as I lifted my arms the wound in my shoulder sent shudders of pain through my body.

Nancy looked at me and rolled her eyes. She stepped forward handing me the book and began feeling the door with both hands while I held the lighter above her. While she did that, I drew my sword and handed it to Leo, seeing as I couldn't put my shoulder into any sort of leverage that would be useful.

The magically inscribed blade wouldn't fit into the seam. After several unsuccessful tries, he handed it back to me and I returned it to my scabbard.

"Now what?" Leo asked.

Before I could answer that I had no idea how we would move forward, Nancy surprised us both by demanding, "Light!"

I brought the lighter in closer and she yanked it from my hand and flicked it back on when the light went out.

"Look!" Nancy hissed the word.

Nancy was indicating a place about a foot and a half higher than my head. It was a symbol with three scratches lines and a circle. One line came down with two running perpendicular and across the seam of the door. Between the two lines rested the circle.

"What is it?" I asked.

"It's in the journal." Nancy snatched it from my hand and handed me back the lighter. I wondered on the remaining fuel in the little firestarter as I held it over Nancy while she flipped through pages of symbols and scribbled notes.

Finally, with confusion in her voice, Nancy said, "I found it, I think."

I looked over her shoulder, and the symbol she was pointing at was definitely the one on the door.

"What do you mean by 'I think'?" I asked.

"Well," Nancy explained, "it means 'thought,' but what would 'thought' be doing written on a door?"

I slapped my forehead and was painfully reminded of the cut I had sustained in the plane crash.

"It's because of the proto-shoggoths!" I exclaimed. "They were telepathic. That was how the Elder Things controlled them."

"What does that have to do with the door?" Leo asked.

I pointed at my head, "Because telepathy will open it!"

Leaning forward I began to gather my will when Nancy and Leo both grabbed my arms.

"What if it's a trap?" Nancy asked. Leo didn't have to say anything. I could tell that he was thinking the same thing.

"Can either of you cast your thoughts?" I demanded.

In their silence I added, "Hardly seems like they would need to set a trap for their slaves and warriors. We're in the proto-shoggoths' tunnels. Nothing would come down here unless it had a death wish."

Before they could argue, I cast out my mind, found the mechanism to unlock the door and gave it a slight mental push.

The door made absolutely no sound as it split and separated with each half retracting into the walls.

"Warriors?" Leo asked.

"What?" I returned.

"You called the shoggoths their warriors."

"Yes," I answered as I tried to peer into the vast darkness that I hoped was the very armory that we had sacrificed so much to get to. "So?"

"They were warriors who were controlled by the Elder Things? Those beasts wielded them like weapons?" Leo continued, but I was only half listening.

"Oh, no." Nancy mumbled as I walked past her.

As soon as my foot touched the floor of the armory, the entire place lit up brighter than any other room that we had been in that day. It was as if the sun itself was shining down on the Antarctic snow before being magnified to fill this chamber.

The room was cylindrical and stretched higher than my eyes

could faithfully see. The diameter of the cylinder was between five and six hundred feet. There were entrances exactly like the one that we came in every ten feet or so. The walls weren't walls at all, but receptacles. Each receptacle held a translucent bubble that was large enough to hold at least three people and was filled with some sort of fluid. They covered the walls entirely, leaving just enough space for the doorways. They stretched all the way up the entirety of the room.

"What is this?" I asked with wonder and excitement in my voice.

"Oh, no." Nancy was whimpering the words at that point and it pulled my attention back to them.

I looked to Leo and his face was paler than his blood loss would have made it.

"Leo, what is it?" I demanded.

He wasn't looking at me, only the pods, as he answered. "Andrew, the proto-shoggoths were the weapons and this is the armory."

It finally clicked in my mind what had them all so terrified, and just as suddenly my wonder and excitement was replaced with just as much terror as my companions had. "This is where the shoggoth sleep." I said.

Nancy's whimpering had lost any resemblance to words and she began to back through the doorway.

"Nancy, wait," I said. She hesitated long enough for me to ask, "The journal said that this is where we would find the means to destroy the city?"

"My father said that," Nancy answered. "He said that the armory would hold the means of destroying the whole continent if we wanted."

"And this is the armory?" I pressed.

Nancy tossed me the journal. "Yes, but he can't be right."

Leo touched her shoulder and she flinched, but recovered enough not to push his hand away.

"Your father was never wrong about these things," Leo said. "He led us here, it must be the right place."

"Stop talking about my father like you knew him!" Nancy shouted it, and the sheer increase in volume startled Leo and me.

...and the armory.

We couldn't see it, but we felt the sudden presence of ... something in there with us.

Nancy shoved Leo in the chest. "See what you did!"

The door slid shut behind us and Nancy spun to me. "Open it!"

I tried to twice, but nothing happened. "No good. We're stuck in here."

She resorted to whimpering again and I didn't blame her.

Leo brought up the machine gun that he had been carrying and readied himself for a battle that I knew we couldn't win.

"What the hell is that?" Nancy asked, and I noticed that the fear in her voice had only ratcheted up.

I looked at where she was pointing. In between two of the pods closer to the floor was a stack of something that was a mix of colors. Browns, reds, yellows, and shades of white were in a heap about as high as my waist.

Leo started to move toward the pile, but I stopped him by grabbing his arm. "Ready your weapon." I said to him.

He readied his machine gun and I drew my pistol choosing to leave the sword inside its scabbard. Nancy held back behind us but close enough to reach. As we inched closer, I think Leo understood what he was looking at before I did. With a smirk he lowered his gun, but continued to walk with me.

Finally, I was close enough to make out what it was.

The browns were Nazi uniforms while the reds, whites, and yellows were the Nazis remains.

Nancy threw up, and Leo just continued to smirk.

"It isn't enough," I said.

"Enough of what?" Leo asked.

"Enough bodies. That's not the entire army."

"It wouldn't be," Nancy returned, wiping her mouth. "This will only be the most nonhuman Germans. The soldiers who could have survived the trip."

I looked around for what might have piled them up.

As I spun, my pistol raised, clapping began.

I aimed my gun at the sound as soon as I registered it.

Command Leader Erich Strobel was walking slowly toward

us with his hands slowly slapping together. "Dr. Andrew Doran! I assumed that it all had to be you." He continued walking toward me, ignoring my raised pistol. "Welcome to my tomb."

"How did you get in here?" Nancy asked from behind Leo and myself.

Strobel stopped clapping and crossed his arms. As he did so, I noticed that he looked disheveled, his coat was unbuttoned halfway down and his stringy white hair was going in every direction.

"My girl, I've been in here for days." He waved his hands around indicating the entirety of the armory. "Haven't you noticed that this place is ... different?"

I took my eyes from the German, knowing that Leo was less curious and more murderous than I was, and examined my surroundings.

I stared at the ceiling that was miles above my head and looked for the nearest place that I could see. Pods and light. I moved my sight down the walls slowly, looking at every detail of the organic pods growing from the walls. Behind the pods was more of the glass-like stone that had made up the rest of the facility. More and more pods. Some of them were translucent, while the others were murky and filled with a milky purple substance. When my eyes came to the floor, I wasn't surprised by what I found. More smooth, black stone.

Leo, who hadn't taken his eyes from Strobel, said, "It's all new."

"What?" I asked. Nancy kept looking at everything and then began nodding.

"None of it is weathered or damaged." She stopped eyeing the walls and turned to face me. "This room hasn't aged."

"Good," said Strobel. "Very good. I am impressed by your companions, Doctor." He smirked and I noticed his teeth were a dingy shade of yellow. "If your gift is for surviving, then your companions have a gift of observation."

I looked at all the doors that were evenly spaced across the cylindrical wall and noticed that they not only looked the same, they were the same. I counted them and there were twenty-four of the identical doors.

"This room is removed from time," I said.

Strobel nodded. "Not only time, but also space. I was chasing you and came in here three days ago, but you just now entered." He stepped closer and Leo jabbed the machine gun in his direction. Strobel got the idea and stopped moving. "You also came in from a different door than I did."

"Why haven't you left?" Nancy asked.

All mirth left Strobel's face. "I was waiting for you."

"What happened to your men?" Leo asked.

Strobel kept staring at Nancy as he answered. "I needed parts."

"Parts?" I asked.

"This room is..." Strobel's face took on an intense look. It was like pain, but he was smiling through it. "...amazing." He grunted the last word.

Strobel's size doubled almost instantly. He didn't move aside from growing, but he really didn't need to. His jaw extended larger than twice the size that it had been, giving him a ridiculous looking underbite that would have been funny if the teeth in his jaw didn't suddenly turn sharper than glass.

"The chamber is for the storage and modification of shoggoths." The mouth on his head hadn't moved, but one had opened up on his neck and was chatting away as he continued to grow. It was only a mouth in that it was a moving slit in his throat that talked, it lacked all other features that would have defined it.

"It was difficult, convincing the Fuhrer that I should be allowed to come along. He wanted to use the alien artifacts, but he didn't like trusting one."

"Alien...?" Nancy was shaking with fear. "You're a ... a..." She raised her gun and started firing. Leo joined suit.

Before I could pull the trigger on my magical .38, Strobel-beast smacked me aside while finishing Nancy's statement.

"I am a Shoggoth!"

He was less man than monster at that point. He stood twelve feet tall, but he wasn't actually standing. Tentacles had shot from his body and he flowed across the floor with a speed that was unmatchable. Strobel's skin had darkened to the same shade of purple that the pods among the walls contained. His body had sprouted mouths and eyes along each of the tentacles. His clothes had completely vanished except for the swastika armband that he seemed to have decided to keep on one of his tentacles.

I hit one of the pods and bounced off it, my pistol sliding well out of my grasp.

Strobel had grown such in size that and tentacles that he was able to reach me from the distance that he had thrown me and still combat Nancy and Leo, whose guns had no visible effect on the monster's girth.

I jumped to my feet and ran at the shoggoth, reaching for my sword as I did. Before I could pull the sword from my scabbard, I was hit by another tentacle and this time I was bitten by one of its many mouths.

I hit the ground on my wounded shoulder and let out a howl. As the pain subsided, I checked the damage to my wrist where the tentacle's teeth bit me and attempted to gain purchase. It was only a graze on my arm and wasn't worth further attention.

Leo landed beside me suddenly and got to his feet much more slowly than I had. His death was still coming and he was starting to feel it. "I have seen shoggoths. He is much bigger than a shoggoth."

"The parts," I answered waving my hand in the direction of the German corpses. "This place allowed him to change his genetic structure to that of a proto-shoggoth. He probably knew how to configure one of the pods and used the body parts for fuel for the transformation."

"Really?" Leo asked.

I shrugged. "I have no idea. It makes sense though."

Strobel was suddenly in front of us and still ignoring Nancy, who had already emptied her gun, collected one from the corpses and was still firing.

One of his tentacles swung at me, but I finally managed to pull my sword before he could hit me. I swung down and the tentacle fell away. He howled as the appendage sizzled with the pain from my magic weapon, but hit both Leo and I with another tentacle before we could prepare for a follow up attack.

We both hit the same pod and spun off toward one of the doors.

I helped Leo to his feet and he grabbed my sword from where it had landed and returned it to me.

"It is too bad," he said through strained breaths, "that we did not know of his agenda before we came here."

"Agreed." I said, and something in his words made a thought begin to form in the back of my mind.

I ignored it and we rushed the Nazi Proto-Shoggoth as it finally began to take notice of Nancy. Leo filled the beast with bullets while I hacked away at it with my sword. While the monster never stopped howling at the pain my sword was causing him, he didn't even feel the bullets from Leo or Nancy's guns.

For all of my cutting and slicing, the Strobel-Shoggoth was healing quicker than my magical sword could damage it. I had never met anything that could stand up to my sword like he was. We were in trouble.

A quick spin of its body and the tentacles launched us all in different directions. I hit the ground and slid into something that jabbed into my back.

I rolled over to find that it was my .38. I was hopeful that my luck had changed.

Back on my feet, I ran at the Strobel-Shoggoth firing until I got close enough to use the sword.

His howling in the physical world echoed deep in my mind, but he was still healing too quickly. He was also getting tired of playing with his food. He smacked me again, but this time I was able to hold onto my weapons.

I landed after bouncing from another pod. As I stood, Nancy grabbed my arm.

"We aren't hurting him!" She was pleading with me.

"We are," I returned. "There just aren't enough of us."

She began whimpering and the idea that Leo had stirred took a slightly more solid shape.

"Nancy, don't focus on that thing anymore. I want you to focus on the doors. Figure out how to get one open."

She began nodding, figuring that I meant we should escape.

I grabbed Nancy by the shoulders and looked her in the eyes. "You tell me the moment that you figure it out!"

Nancy nodded again, but just stood there.

"Go!" I shouted it more roughly that I probably should have, but I was fairly sure that we were going to all die and all niceties had flown out of the window at that point.

Nancy took off toward the nearest door and I reloaded my pistol. Instead of firing it, because I was hoping that the Plan B I was having Nancy work on would pan out, I holstered it and ran at the Strobel-Shoggoth with my sword raised.

Each time a tentacle came at me, I managed to get the blade in the way. I wasn't hacking any more limbs off because he could grow them back too quickly, but the blade hurt him enough to keep making his tentacles back off every time he touched it.

Leo had scooped up two more Nazi machine guns and was firing a continuous stream at the monster. Even with this non-stop pummel of bullets entering his hide, the Strobel-Shoggoth only had eyes for me.

That was why I was taken completely by surprise when Leo let out a gasp of pain.

I looked to my friend and saw a horrific sight. As I had blocked the tentacles that threatened to toss or maim me, Leo had been open to being speared by one directly through his previous gun wounds.

A large black tentacle, with mouths gnawing at his insides, was completely through him, its tip protruding from his back by about three feet.

I screamed in defiance for my friend and hacked two limbs out of my way as I ran to his side. I could hear a throbbing noise echoing from the Strobel-Shoggoth and through my mind.

He was laughing.

I cut his laughter off by literally cutting off the tentacle that was in my friend.

It withered and fell from him. Leo collapsed.

Leo kept firing at the beast as I lowered him to the smooth floor and into a puddle of his own blood.

"I am surprised by the lack of pain," Leo said.

I shook my head. "That's the spell from earlier." I looked

at the growing puddle as Leo continued to fire at the Strobel-Shoggoth. It was easy to see that he was trying to keep it off me while I was distracted. "The spell won't be able to hold in your blood any more." I looked at the hole. It was about three inches wide and despite what I had just said, his blood was only trickling out of it.

"I cannot watch your back with only guns," Leo said. "Fight it."

My friend was right and I tightened my grip on my sword and turned to face it.

Leo grabbed my arm, letting one of the guns fall.

"Fight it and win."

I nodded and gathered my will.

Reaching to the void, I blocked each of the incoming tentacles with the magic that I had access to and came in low with my blade. I tried to carve off pieces of the creature, but he was simply too fast.

Keeping the tentacles at bay with my mind, I tried different tactics with my magic. I tried to hold it still, but it was too strong. I tried to pull it towards me, but it was quick enough to slide by me.

At one point, I even tried pulling the pods from the wall to hurl at it, but once again he was fast enough to avoid the popping sac of slime and membrane.

Forcing myself to fall into and out of the void, I tried to disappear and reappear in different places to surprise it with different attacks. I managed to keep the Strobel-Shoggoth surprised, but he was once again healing too quickly for me to destroy.

Finally, as if waiting for me to run out of ideas, Nancy shouted, "I've got it!"

I put all of my power into throwing the monster back and away from myself and my path to Nancy. Sending a quick glance to Leo, I noted that he was alive, although fading fast, before sprinting to Nancy's side.

"It's incredibly simple." she said while watching over my shoulder as the beast sped toward us. "Um," she was terrified, but kept going. "It is still a mental trigger. You were pushing when you came in here, so now you have to pull." Nancy looked at me with tears streaming down her face. "Does that make sense?"

I was already touching my magic, so I sent a wave out to the door in the manner that I thought the young Dyer girl meant, and it slid open silently. "Bingo!" I shouted.

I turned to Nancy and grabbed her by the shoulders. "Don't stop moving, keep it behind you and try to stay ahead of it. Use your gun." I looked back at the creature almost on top of us. "I'll kill it, but you have to keep it busy."

Terror, more than I had seen her express up to that point, filled her eyes. "Wait! You're leaving? Why? Where?"

I ran through the door and shouted, "To get reinforcements!"

Before Nancy could follow, I sent another pulse of my will at the door and it slid shut.

I stopped as soon as the door shut, and I turned back toward it, hoping this would work. I pushed my will at the door again and stepped through.

The view had changed completely.

Instead of Nancy standing beside the door and the Strobel-Shoggoth speeding at me, the Strobel-Shoggoth was speeding away from me. I was on the opposite side of the chamber from where I had left.

On the far side of the armory, I saw Nancy crying and talking to another me. As she spoke the door directly behind that me slid open. He said another few words and then ran through the door. It slid closed behind him and Nancy began pounding on it, not listening to the words I had just said to her.

"Dammit, Nancy!" I shouted at the top of my lungs. "When I tell you to run," I drew my pistol and fired into the back of the Strobel-Shoggoth as quickly as my trigger finger could pump, "I mean 'Run'!"

Nancy and the monster both spun in confusion. Nancy's face was priceless. She had absolutely no idea what I had just done. Even better was the monster's face. While shoggoth expressions weren't easy to read by human standards, I had lots of experience and he looked shocked.

I kept firing until I was out of bullets. Then I stopped and took my time reloading. The monster began sliding at me with his incredible speed. Before he got within striking distance to me, another bullet from another magical .38 hit it in the side of the bulbous mass that had once been Erich Strobel's face.

"Dammit, Nancy!" The other me, who had just entered through another door, said. "How many times do I have to tell you?"

Nancy seemed to at least accept what she was seeing, if not understand it. She took off running. As she ran by each door, it slid open and another me, a little more battle-weary than the last, stepped in, smiled at her and fired at the Strobel-Shoggoth.

By the time she made it to, well, the first me to enter the arena, I had finished loading my gun. Nancy stopped and, panting, asked me how.

"This room stands outside of time. Strobel wanted to beat me here, and he did. By three days." I shrugged. "Proto-Shoggohs, the originals, not this abomination, were telepathic. I willed myself to enter into the fight at the moment that I left." I paused. "And it looks like I might have to do it twenty-four more times."

The other Andrew Dorans were converging on the Strobel-Shoggoth. As hundreds of magical .38 bullets entered the beast's flesh, it blackened to a different shade. It was a shade that I had seen many times on creatures from the void. It was the shade of my bullets killing it.

"If you'll excuse me," I said to Nancy and moved toward the monster, firing as I walked.

Once I had reached the Strobel-Shoggoth, several other Andrew Dorans were already close enough to start hacking away at it.

Within moments the beast was nothing but a puddle on the floor.

I moved toward the door that I had come from and twenty-two of the other Andrews did the same. One stayed.

The last one.

I knelt down beside Leo. His death was soon in coming and I had one last favor to offer him.

Nancy knelt beside us both. She was holding his hand and

sobbing with the force of a person who had seen too many horrors for one day.

"How can the armory destroy the city?" Leo asked.

I shook my head. "It can't."

Through her sobbing, Nancy said, "Father said that it could."

"The Nazis were headed here, and your father said something else to me as well, back in the Blasted Heath. I thought that he was telling me about how he was keeping his mind safe, but I think he was actually telling me about this place."

Leo mouthed the word, "What?"

I grabbed his hand. "First things first." His eyes started to close, so I slapped him across the face. "Do you want to live?"

Leo coughed up blood, but nodded, hope filling his eyes.

I gave Leo a look that I knew he understood. "It will be ... different."

He acknowledged the look with a look of his own, paused, and then nodded.

I placed my hand over his eyes and began to chant.

Leo woke up on a cot to me sitting beside him.

Quickly he lifted his shirt and felt his abdomen. There wasn't a mark there. No holes from bullets or tentacles.

Sitting up, Leo looked around at his surroundings. "Where are we?" As far as my ears could tell, his accent was completely gone.

We sat in a cabin with almost no furniture. The windows each showed a different season. A young blond child was leaning against the wall.

"Am I in your Dream Lands?" Leo asked me.

I nodded. "Your body was beyond repair. It was here or death."

Leo nodded. "What can I do in the land of make-believe?"

The ancient child answered Leo's question. "There are many monsters here to be fought, but I think Dr. Doran has a different idea for you."

Leo looked at the child with the ancient eyes and then to me. "Do you?"

I nodded again. "When I needed to know where Dyer was,

I came here. This land is useful for keeping eyes on information that is sometimes harder to acquire. If you're not against remaining my assistant, I could use you here."

Leo nodded slowly. "Can I think on it?" He looked around. "I have a feeling that this place will take much time to get used to."

"Time moves different here," the child and I said at the same time.

The ancient child stepped forward. "There is a girl, in the city, that you will meet. I will take you to her and she will teach you about the world. She will do so because she feels a strong kinship with Dr. Doran." He was standing beside the bed now. "But there is a cost."

"I told him that you wouldn't mind as long as it wasn't too high," I added.

Leo looked from me, there was distrust in his eyes, but not for me. It was for this child that I had described to him before. "What price?"

"You will also work for me," the child answered. "There are many things that you will come across as you learn of the Dream Lands, but I need knowledge of your world that you come from." He waved a hand at me. "Dr. Doran has given me the ability to visit your former world, yet it has changed too much since I have been there. I wish to learn of it so that I may blend in during my visits."

Leo nodded and smiled, "I think that I can handle that cost."

The ancient child nodded. "I will leave you both to your farewells."

The child went to the door of his home and left.

I stood up.

"You're just going to leave me here?" Leo asked, a hint of hurt in his voice.

"You're not dead, and we both have a lot of work to do." I was sad at my friend's transition, but hid it.

Leo stood and nodded. "I will miss our war." He thrust out his hand to receive a handshake.

I shook his hand firmly and said, "Our war is still raging, and soon you'll be a formidable tool in it again."

I flipped him a coin. "If you need anything, say the word 'Fthagn,' while holding the coin and I will hear it and come as soon as possible."

I approached the door the ancient child had left through. "Be careful, Andrew Doran. Without me by your side, who will watch your back?"

"The position," I replied, "has already been filled."

After I had delivered Leo to the Dream Lands, he had remained there, unconscious for days in Dream Land time. That had given me enough time to find the original location of the Nazis staging area.

The cavern was only guarded by two remaining soldiers. The rest must have been dragged into the employ of Strobel's genetic experiments. I dispatched them both quickly and carried every explosive that I could find into the tunnels that led to the armory.

After those tunnels had been collapsed sufficiently enough to wake the dead, I gathered Nancy and we left.

For her benefit, we attempted to locate the body of Nancy's father, but something had taken William and we both agreed, albeit reluctantly, that trying to find him was too dangerous.

Nancy showed me where the Nazis had entered the caverns and we left that same way. Two more soldiers, both Yig cultists, were guarding the trucks.

I didn't even bother dispatching them, because only a Nazi Shoggoth would be stupid enough to drag cold-blooded Yig worshippers to Antarctica.

We drove back to the shore and it took most of the night. Once we arrived, we were blessed with a sight that we hadn't expected to see.

When word had traveled through the channels of prayer worship to Dagon's children that some of his less-loved offspring were marooned and surrounded by underwater enemies (the submarine), fishmen had flocked to dispatch of them.

Not knowing how to deal with the fishmen trying to pry open their hull, the Nazis retreated to a safe radio distance from the shore.

The fishmen had also brought with them a small steamboat. It wouldn't get us or Sebastian's men far, but it didn't have to. We only needed to get to Hobart, Tasmania.

Nancy never left my side, which surprised me. She kept busy by cleaning guns, reading more of her father's journal, and writing in her own.

Once we were in Hobart, I asked one of Sebastian's closest friends, Eliza Allen, if there was any word on the Nazi sub.

"I hear that it's on a course with South Africa," Eliza answered.

I frowned. "That's hardly the correct direction."

Eliza shrugged. "Once they failed to receive response from their people, they must have received new orders." She left me with that.

I sat down in a restaurant near the harbor and tried to figure out my next move.

I could return to Miskatonic. Carol would be livid by now and I still had to sign those documents on the building ... or reconstruction ... or something.

Except that I couldn't get my mind off why the Nazis would be traveling to South Africa. There was nothing for them to gain there.

Suddenly, the chair across from me was filled with an excited Nancy Dyer.

"I think I know why they went to South Africa," she said.

I was both confused and curious. "Why?"

Nancy slammed her father's journal down. "Do you know what the Book of Eibon is?"

I frowned. "A book of powerful magic and black arts. It only exists in incomplete translations. The original text lost to the ages."

Nancy rested her hand on the book. "My father thought that the original text was somewhere in South Africa."

My eyes shot wide. "Did he say where?"

She shook her head. "Only vague directions that he translated from over 200 years ago. It would take some work to find."

I nodded slowly. What else had Brandon Smythe shared

with the Nazis? This was definitely possible.

Smiling, I said, "I recently had a job opening for a gun-toting assistant. Would you perhaps be interested in the position?"

Nancy frowned. She had suffered so much since she had met me, but she had also had her eyes opened so very wide in that time.

"How's the pay?"

"Horrible, and there's the potential that you might lose your mind" I replied, and then added, "Free room and board, though. And lots of travel."

Nancy gave a little half smile. "I am not sure how I will do as 'gun-toting,' but I am willing to give it a shot." Her smile spread the rest of the way and she added, "Besides, I think I know more about your pistol than you do. I'm sure you would like to hear that story."

"I would think that you're right," I replied and stood up. "Then I think that we need to find transport to South Africa."

Note from the author:

We greatly appreciate you taking the time to read our work. Please consider leaving a review wherever you bought the book, or telling your friends about *Andrew Doran at the Mountains of Madness*, to help us spread the word. Thank you so much for your support.

That being said: This book was made possible by the support of fans, friends, and family.

Thank you,
Ren Davenport
Parker Waddell
Rachel Eliason
Maria Sanchez
Bryan Smithers
Jessica Vavrasek
Sidney Zellmer
Janeea Choiniere
Sarah McCarter
Dana Saffran
Patricia Wilson
Melissa Bartels
Nate Goodman
Adam Jacobs
David Hambling
Greg Kischer
Mary Hamby-Collins
Kurt Sparks
Lori Hunt
Ryan Parker
Andrew Blackmon
Dana Beatty

About the Author

Matthew Davenport lives in Des Moines, Iowa with his beautiful wife, Ren. He spends his time writing, reading, and working to promote and support writing communities in Iowa through his company Davenport Writes, LLC.

You can keep track of Matthew through his twitter account @spazenport. You can follow his blog at http://authormatthew-davenport.wordpress.com

Bibliography:

Novels:

Random Stranger (Abstract Series 1)
Stranger Books (Abstract Series 2)
The Statement of Andrew Doran
Andrew Doran at the Mountains of Madness
Broken Nights
Broken Nights: Strange Worlds
The Sons of Merlin
The Trials of Obed Marsh

Curious about other Crossroad Press books?
Stop by our site:
http://store.crossroadpress.com
We offer quality writing
in digital, audio, and print formats.

Enter the code FIRSTBOOK
to get 20% off your first order from our store!
Stop by today!

CPSIA information can be obtained
at www.ICGtesting.com
Printed in the USA
LVHW081925121119
637136LV00012B/1152/P

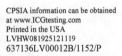